HAITI'S NIGHTMARE 2010

BY BOBBY KISSOON

authorHOUSE®

AuthorHouse™
1663 Liberty Drive
Bloomington, IN 47403
www.authorhouse.com
Phone: 1 (800) 839-8640

Published by AuthorHouse 06/21/2016

ISBN: 978-1-5246-1522-2 (sc)
ISBN: 978-1-5246-1521-5 (e)

Print information available on the last page.

Any people depicted in stock imagery provided by Thinkstock are models, and such images are being used for illustrative purposes only. Certain stock imagery © Thinkstock.

This book is printed on acid-free paper.

DEDICATED TO;

All my books are specially dedicated to my ever loving sisters;
the late Rita of New Ansterdan, and Helina of Guyana. Meena
of Canada. Seeta of Palmiste, and Sunita of La Romain,
Trinidad. And so is my loving wife Joyce from Texas.

Introduction

It was February 12, 2010 on the calendar, as the hands of the clock struck 4 pm the island of Haiti in the Caribbean Sea was battling to stay above the surface of the water, while the inhabitants were fighting for survival.

It was like a boat in the Atlantic ocean hit by high waves, trembling while every thing inside was crumbling so was Haiti. The large and enormous concrete buildings were in the hands of nature, man had built them but at present God was shaking mother earth to show everyone who is more powerful.

All those who were at present on that island began to shout for God, for some it was their first time they had prayed from the bottom of their heart. The neighbouring island could feel the effect of the trembling of the earth-quake that measured 7.0 on the mega scale.

A few minutes later the news began to spread like wildfire through the telephone lines and the satellite, demanding help from the people of this land of Haiti.

Within a few hours the people of the entire universe on earth began to cry, their heart began to develop a feeling of love as their eyes began to shed tears to show the real meaning of love for human beings should be bound in unity of love as God had thought us through all his scriptures that had been written by men as his servants.

As such every one was eager to help in some ways, but million of miles kept them apart. Instead all they could do was to offer prayers to the Lord almighty to have mercy upon those souls and people of Haiti.

However, by nightfall in Haiti it was like a lost battlefield where the war is over leaving the survivours to take care of their casualties and dead, while the victorious army had left with victory.

Ironically the powerful and wealthy nations of the world were putting things together to help those helpless who were at present in pains and agony nursing their wounds, without a shelter and electricity yet depending on nature, the moon for light, "Oh God please help them."

Chapter 1

In the dark of the silent night there were cries of pain everywhere. Some were pinned below rubble and debris, while others were buried alive. Hence, love among families was destroyed while the world at large could hear the cries in the atmosphere ringing in their ears. Some could see it in visions. It was so lachrymose!

As the intense earthquake ended, leaving the island in turmoil, the world's superpower, the United States of America, decided to send the largest warship in the world to help with the casualties. This warship had sailed on the water of mother earth on her first voyage to Afghanistan to destroy the Muslim terrorists and restore peace for the people of the Middle East.

The ship's second errand was to the West Indies to a Caribbean island that God had destroyed named Haiti. Its purpose was to provide help. On board this warship was a young army doctor named Dale Mackintyre. Dale was born and raised in Tennessee. At the age of twenty-five, he was recruited as a doctor in the US Army. As such, he was one of the young doctors on board the largest navy ship in the world on its first voyage to the Middle East. On this second expedition, Dr. Dale was approaching his thirtieth year.

Dr. Dale Mackintyre was tall at six and a half feet in height. He had a medium build and the features of a world heavyweight boxer. He was very handsome, with a short, combed-back hairstyle and a mat of black hair above a face as round as an apple. But in his career as an army doctor there were no females to admire him, so he remained a bachelor.

Dale's father, Steve Mackintyre, was a farmer in Tennessee. He met his wife, Dolly, there. They became the parents of three children. Dale was the eldest, then a daughter, Stacy, who became a schoolteacher, and then at last David, a lawyer from the Bar Association.

Steve Mackintyre had inherited some land from his parents. Being a hardworking man, he bought out a few of his neighbours so at last he owned an estate with a few farmhouses, along with his agricultural equipment and farmhands.

Dr. Dale grew up on these lands. As a child in his spare time after school, he worked as a farm hand, so he was exposed to a hard way of life. On television, his favorite movies were westerns and war movies, so his idea of adventure was to become a soldier. After his university studies in medicine, he became a soldier by joining the US Army, where he was placed on the largest warship in the world, which was docked in the waters of the Caribbean near Haiti.

Obviously, the entire world wanted to help, while some wanted to visit—not to help but to explore and make money, being a plague on helpless individuals. These were the terriorists with their own ideas, along with the media and their cameras.

Among a television crew from Britain's BBC was a pretty young lady by the name of Britney Hudson—a journalist. Britney was twenty-five years old. She was pretty and as proud as the flying flag of England. She stood six full feet in height, with golden, curly hair to her shoulder with a well-carved face and a curvy body. She looked like a child's doll. As such, she was proud of her job and her beauty.

Britney was the only child of an English army captain, Anderson Hudson, and fashion model, Emily Hudson. Britney had traveled to many countries for her career—like her mother and father did for their careers—but Britney told herself her beauty always made her job easy. She charmed everyone's eyes, especially young males, whom she always took advantage of.

This devastated island was laden with miseries and pains, and there were many intruders who visited for their own purpose. Like the Hudsons, they were all preparing something for this island. Captain Anderson got word from his superior to prepare his battalion to travel to Haiti to help as a rescue team, while Emily and her colleagues were busy organizing and preparing to raise money to help in some way, either with food or medicine. Britney was flying with her media team immediately to let the world see what was going on in this distressed land.

Within hours of the earthquake, Britney and her team were in the air heading for their destination.

Relaxing in a luxurious aircraft, Britney imagined past adventures in her career, from being on the battlefield among soldiers to viewing terrorist attacks throughout the world, to interviewing celebrities living in luxury. When she placed herself among them, life seemed to be strange and a challenge to some, while to others life was just a burden of pains, as it was with this destination. She flew regularly to different countries. It made her sick to her stomach. She just wanted to find a handsome husband and turn her back against this hostile world and live with her lover on some romantic island. Then she would become a writer of novels about her experiences and one day might win a prize and become as famous as one of those celebrities she interviewed.

At last her thoughts were interrupted as their aircraft was about to touch down at their destination of pain to air the sufferings of these helpless people.

Chapter 2

This devastated island was like a recent battlefield. Buildings were smashed to the ground, while smoke was oozing in the air from small infernos. These buildings had caught fire due to the electricity. On the streets, dead bodies were lying everywhere. Some casualities were screaming in pain while survivors were busy rescuing trapped individuals.

The activities of the volunteers and survivors were different. It was like a chain of movements—like bees or ants. Britney was busy with the microphone echoing her sweet voice, while her cameraman was busy with his camera so that the people in England and elsewhere could look upon the conditions the horrible island was presently facing.

Dr. Dale and his team of soldiers had pitched a tent in the road. The American soldiers formed their own rescue team, while Dale and a few other doctors were busy tending to the casualties. The time was moving so fast that everyone was getting tired, but looking at human beings crying in pain for some sort of help, the volunteers did not feel their tiredness.

It was about five o'clock in the morning. Two American soldiers brought in a young girl of about sixteen years on a stretcher to Dr. Dale's medical camp. Lying on the stretcher in front of Dr. Dale, this young girl was in pain and half naked, almost nude. This was because the volunteers tried their best to get her from under some rubble. However, her clothes were torn apart.

Dr. Dale treated her for the pain she was suffering from. Then he realized she was almost nude and there was no one by her side to cover her nakedness. So he pulled off his army T-shirt and put it on this victim leaving, himself half naked.

Journalist Britney Hudson was doing her job but was distracting other young male volunteers. She had on a tight-fitting jeans with a pair of high heels. To cover her upper body she had on a short T-shirt that clung to her body. She wore this because she would be on the television regularly to answer questions from other journalists, so she must look attractive to her millions of viewers.

Britney was enjoying this, for she knew that all the young male soldiers' eyes were on her, tired and fatigued, pretty Britney.

Then at 6:00 in the morning the aftershock of the earthquake once more began to show its power. Buildings once more began to crumble. Those that were halfway crumbled began to fall apart. Boulders began to roll down the hills.

Britney's team began to run for cover. Britney, with her heels and tight-fitting jeans, was not very agile. A few boulders were faster than her. Those boulders were bouncing like a cricket ball to the batsman, so pretty Britney Hudson fell to the ground. Britney lay unconscious on the street of Port au Prince, Haiti, as an earthquake victim. Her cell phone and microphone disappeared, just like her cameraman had gone his way to seek cover.

Dr. Dale and his colleagues ran and left their tents as they began to vibrate in a dancing motion. Everyone was in the clear, trying to protect themselves. This nightmare of an experience faded within a few minutes, but everyone's hearts were jumping out of their trembling bodies.

The earth's powerful movements came to a standstill at last. This resulted in more casualties and fewer helpers. A new era began with screams, some for help and others in pain. Britney's team had scattered. She was picked up by two American soldiers and placed on their stretcher. By her side was her cameraman, Bill Samson. Bill was in his mid-thirties. He was about five feet three inches tall, and he was fat, with a big belly. He was bald and wore a pair of glasses, with a thick moustache below his nose.

As the two American soldiers were moving quickly toward their medical camp, Bill Samson was close at their heels with his camera on his shoulder.

By this time Dale and his companions were once again busy, the two American soldiers brought Britney directly to Doctor Dale table, being a white female in position she was liable for preference rather than the Haitians.

Seeing Britney Doctor Dale gave a sharp whistle, as he asked.

"Soldiers, where you found this morning rose?"

"She is my reporter!" Answered Bill.

"She is a journalist?" asked Dale.

"Yes, we are working for the BBC" answered Bill.

"OK let wake her up to hear her sweet voice" Said Doctor Dale.

"That is why we brought her to you Doctor" said Bill

Dale looked at Bill then said "Get that camera man out this tent"

"Are you a soldier or a doctor" asked Bill.

Dale gave Bill a serious look in his face and said, "No camera is allowed in my camp".

"Doctor, why don't you find some clothes to cover that body of a monster" said Bill as he walked out of the tent.

Britney was laid on Doctor Dale's operation table, her white t-shirt became brown and black with the debris, and she had a few bruises on her skin that leaved a few drops of blood on her t-shirt. Doctor Dale plucked off her t-shirt to examine her body, he then tossed the dirty t-shirt to a nurse and said "Nurse some national of victims may need this, take care of it"

He then loosen Britney tight jeans for better blood circulation then said to a nurse "Nurse get me a bottle of drinking water please"

He then took out his pocket handkerchief wet it with water to wipe away the dust from Britney's face and body. Doctor Dale was an experienced doctor in this position, not wanting to waste any medical substance in a position like this, he decided to do a body resuscitation. So taking his two hands together he gently began to press the left side of Britney breast to massage the heart. He then opened her mouth and began to pump oxygen from his breath to her lungs. He got no result; once again he began to press her left breast gently as a quick jerk.

He got result, Britney began to slowly breathe, he then thought to himself to pump more oxygen to her lungs. As he was forcing air down Britney's lungs from his mouth Britney gain conscious, she opened her eyes to see a bareback huge male over her face. At this same time Doctor Dale release Britney's lips to suck in more oxygen from the air, he once again placed his mouth on Britney's lips.

Britney in pre consciousness hit him a hard slap and shove him away from her body. She then struggle for a sitting position. Then realized her conditions of being half naked then her jeans bottoms had been loosened, she tried to cover her breasts with her two hands, it all happened so fast, then she shouted in a hoarse voice, "What the hell is going on."

Doctor Dale stood back looking at her.

Doctor Dale was trying to re-juvenate you, princess." said a nurse.

Doctor Dale companion was looking on whose name was doctor Boxton.

Dale looked at doctor Boxton with smile on his face and said to him, "Pal, please give that morning star your t-shirt so that she could cover her beauty the sun is up."

Without hesitation doctor Boxton plucked off his army t shirt and toss it to Britney she snapped it in the air and began to scramble inside it.

Britney then looking at Doctor Dale in a confused state could see her stale lipstick on his lips, then said, "Like the American government do not have money to clothe their soldiers"

"Yes of course, the American army has enough clothes for his people, but they had given their personal clothing in charity to certain female like your nakedness in a time like this" said Nurse Stella.

Britney in embarrassment looked at Doctor Dale handsome face as his eyes were piercing her. He then gave her a smile and said "Are you ok, beautiful?"

"Yes I am fine, except for a few scratches" answered Britney.

"OK nurse Stella will patch you up, this is no hospital for rest." said Doctor Dale as he turned away to tend to a waiting casualties.

Nurse Stella with haste began to put a few patches of bandages on Britney's hands and body when there were cuts and bruises.

"Is he a graduate Doctor or some Soldier Vet?" asked Britney.

"He is a graduate medical doctor who joined the army to serve his people and others who need his help." said Nurse Stella.

"So his wife is a soldier or a Doctor?" asked Britney.

"He is a bachelor" said Stella

"That is why he tried to kiss me." said Britney.

"He brought you back to life, by trying to help you." said Stella.

"What happened to his clothes?" asked Britney.

"A short while ago a young girl came in nude, he tended to her, then cover her nakedness with his clothes as the other doctor had done to you." said Stella.

"Oh God, by the way how come I end up in this situation?" asked Britney.

"After the aftershock this morning two of our soldiers brought you here, your cameraman is outside" said Stella.

"Oh my God, but is he with me?" asked Britney.

"Yes as you walk out the camp you will see your Bill with his camera" said Stella.

At last Britney Hudson was helped to her feet once more where she was joined by her mate Bill Samson.

Chapter 3

Abu-Farouk Mohammed, a young and handsome terrorist at present was stalking Miss Britney Hudson and her father Captain Anderson Hudson of the British Army.

Abu was in his late twenties a few years older than Britney, but he was so handsome that any young woman could fall an easy victim to his prey. He was six feet tall with wide shoulders, a neatly carved face with a charming smile, at present he was more handsome than any Indian movie star. His charm, intellect and activities were developed by his father and his terrorist organization.

This young terrorist who graduated from various universities in the world for his father was a millionaire in Afghanistan.

Abu Sherriff Mohammed was a businessman in Afghanistan, he had helped to finance Saddam Hussain into power, so as Saddam gained power money and wealth was his dreams, he had so much money that he had no use of, so he once began to finance the Al Qaeda terrorists.

He had six wives in six different countries living in luxuries. Abu Farouk's mother Farida hailed from Pakistan, she was sixteen years of age when Sheriff Mohammed saw her in Pakistan, with Sheriff's power he made her his sixth wife, and there he built a mansion for her.

At this young age Farida could not conceive a child according to the doctors, so he spent a few millions dollars for the doctors to fertilize her eggs with his sperms, as a result Abu Farouk Mohammed was born, he was a million dollars child, and he was Sherriff last child.

Abu Farouk Mohammed job for his father was to work as a spy, as a cover up he was one of his agent in promoting his business throughout the world. This young man had graduated in law, a medical doctor and a university certificate in science so all instrument in a lab was a toy for him such was the human body then he knew the law well, this made his father Abu Sheriff Mohammed a Billion dollars insurance policy.

At present Abu Farouk Mohammed, had landed on this island with his team as soon the news was spread. As the leader on his mission of this propetuity island, he and his terriorist cabal came here for a reason, the reason to make billions of dollars. But was in disguide of a donor and helper to the Haitian people. He had a group of terrorists orginisation, working as pioneers volunteers and Red Cross in name of his father. For Farouk and his team to be in Haiti spending all these money was a trap to a special prey.

Abu and his team had landed on this island over night with an billion dollar water plane, it brought the main items, to set up his operation, in the mean while there will be his over all team in operation within a few days. ''THE ANGEL OF DEATH'' will be here soon! Every thing they owned were expensive with its value. To this team to be here, these were some of Abu and his team missions.

On the other hand, there were many other resque operations, one such was the world's largest warship will be afloat in the Haitian waters, secondly Captain Anderson Hudson of the English Army had destroyed some key power in Afghanistan, the other reason was to help the helpless people in Haiti and convert them in to Muslims then later on their will be a cult of Muslim terrorists in Haiti working for Sherriff Mohammed. Most important Miss Britney Hudson must be a victim to Abu Farouk Mohammed for revenge to destroyed England as the roll they played in the fall of President Saddam Hussain and his followers who were sheriff's friends.

Farouk Mohammed had met Britney in Afghanistan in 2004, during the War with America joined England to capture Saddam Hussain's regime. He had encountered with Britney as a lawyer for some of his colleagues, but was not interested over her beauty or profession, because he was of a higher quality but as times goes by his terrorist group found out that she was the daughter of Captain Anderson Hudson.

It was then lay out by these terrorist, that in his next encounter with Britney he would have to act as an intelligent play boy to achieve his goal, to hold on to Britney and use her as his toy to get his job done, then he will dump her in some way which was no problem for a terrorist. They will make some money out of her in their business that will unfold later.

Ironically intelligent Abu Farouk Mohammed set up his camp outside the town of Port au Prince to a well known village named St. Mark. This was their base and foundation in Haiti. The terrorist had planted a tree in Haiti, for here it will grow and give shelter and at last the work of Farouk and his team, his second in command at present was Doctor Fizal Khan from Afghanistan, he had already sent hundreds of suicide bombers to their death, taking hundreds of thousands of innocent lives with them.

Captain Anderson Hudson and his battalion of sergeants, corporals and lieutenants, doctors, nurses and soldiers arrived on an English Army private jet. They were fully equipped for their mission; they arrived a day later and pitch their camp in Port Au Prince.

Britney mother Emily and her friends, Joshua show models and her company had prepared some bundles of clothing of all sizes both male and female, but most of the clothing were t-shirts with Emily photograph and her companions also some of Britney's photos too. This Captain Anderson had in his command for disposal.

Arriving on the island of Haiti Captain Anderson command began as they started their own business. Their camp was pitched, soldiers went in search of casualties brought them in for treatments, so they were sharing their own food supplies and clothing.

In the streets of Haiti there were nationalities of all languages from distant developed countries, all trying to help and show love to their fellow human beings, everyone was busy as the bees or the ants a little rest and back to work as for some hands closing two days and nights without a nap. Inside of their heart was love to help regardless of their tiredness, but regardless of their sufferings of the victims they wanted to help.

On the second day of Captain Hudson arrival on this island, on his whereabouts he noticed the American army based camp, so he decided to pay a visit for he had joined forces many times in Afghanistan, so majority of the soldiers are known friends to the British soldiers, inside the medical camp he met with Doctor Dale Mackintyre. Dale is a good friend of Captain Hudson, on a front line battle with the Muslim terrorist in Afghanistan.

Captain Hudson was shot by his enemies and was rushed to the US army camp that was closest for medical treatment, his condition was critical, so he was sent on board the American warship for medication, there Doctor Dale was his doctor as such they became good friends as soldiers fighting together.

In the US army camp in Haiti Captain Hudson had some brief handshake, but was invited by Doctor Dale to join him the said evening on board the US army warship to his cabin. In the evening both of them decided that they would be available, so some expensive liquor would settle their stomach after all theses pains and fatigue, also on the war ship there would be more of Captain Hudson friends. Above all Captain Hudson had accepted Doctor Dale's invitation to his cabin for a drink.

After lunch time that said day Captain Hudson met his daughter miss Britney Hudson they met as usual on most battlefield, Britney as a journalist and Hudson a soldier, it was their job unlike home as father and daughter. After a brief handshake between daughter and father, Captain said:

"Are you free this evening?"

"Kind of busy, is there any importance, I could make some time for you dad" said Britney.

"I would like to take you on board the world's largest warship afloat on the sea owned by the American" said Captain Hudson.

"I would like to Dad!" said Britney.

"Well make some time!" said Hudson.

"Are you an invited guest or on business with those Americans?" asked Britney.

"They are our friends" said Hudson.

"Dad will they accept me on their ship?" asked Britney.

"I am invited by a friend of mine by the name of Doctor Dale Mackintyre, also I will like to meet some other friends onboard" answered Captain Hudson.

"Young Doctor Dale?" asked Britney.

"Yes, he is a young man, have you known him from somewhere" said Captain Hudson.

"Yes! After the shock yesterday, he treated me, he look like some cow boys kind of doctor" said Britney.

"What do you mean, a cow boy doctor, he is a good doctor he save my life a few years in Afghanistan, there we became friends" said Captain Hudson.

"Yesterday when he tends to me, he was in need of a shirt, he was bareback like some vagrant" said Britney.

"OK my daughter, he is a gentle man, I know him well as a friend, further more your mother had sent some shirts with yours and hers photographs on them, may be you could give him one or two so he could have some clothes on" said Hudson.

"Ok I will see you about six this evening and by the way thank you for the invitation." said Britney as they separated for both were busy.

Before the sun could hide itself behind the horeizon of those high hills of Haiti, Britney was by her father Captain Hudson camp. Britney took a few her t-shirts from a bundle, one of hers photo the other of her mother, she wrapped them in a parcels to make a gift, within minutes she was by her father side in an army jeep while Captain Hudson driving towards the Caribbean sea where the American warship was docked.

By the time the sun had hid itself behind the high hill and the moon began to show its beauty on this island with out any electricity, looking at the island was some small glare of some kind of oil lamp or some small fire build for heat by the inhabitants.

On the various army or Red Cross or some volunteers camp the noise of generators could be heard too for some light. That was the only beauty, some places as volunteers wearing head lights for their job it was like candle flies moving about. Above all the sea surrounding the island looked pretty with all the ships lights.

Due to Captain Anderson Hudson familiarities among the American soldiers, his identification was not put in use, so without any problem they were on board the American warship, but it take some times for the Captain and his beautiful daughter could reach Doctor Dale's cabin. Inside the warship there was already a heavy crowded hospital with casualties who needed urgent operation to save their lives, the entire ship was busy, but yet the Captain had stopped for a handshake and a few words.

After sometime they were shown to a cabin on top deck, of a door marked "Doctor Dale" Captain Hudson gave a few fast light rap with the back of his index finger, then a voice from inside answered "Who is it?"

"Captain Hudson" replied Captain Hudson.

Within a few seconds the cabin door was open from inside by Doctor Dale.

Doctor Dale had just finished taken a bathe so he had his towel wrapped around his waist to cover his underwear, for this was an army ship and his visitors supposed to be a male soldier so he open the door while his guest will be comfortable seated he will get himself in some clothing, but this was not what he had been expecting.

As Dale's visitors enter his cabin, Captain Hudson followed by his daughter Britney, Dale looked in astonishment, his and Britney eyes were fixed on one another. The silence was interrupted by Hudson.

"Doctor Dale please meet my daughter miss Britney Hudson"

"I met her already" said Dale as he shook Mr. Hudson hands then Britney's

As Doctor Dale came to his realization of his conditions, he briskly said

"Please excuse me, miss … sir … so I could put on some clothes" with a smile on his handsome face.

"That's fine we will make ourselves comfortable as you get your self dress young man" said Captain Hudson.

Britney handed Doctor Dale the parcels with the two t-shirts and said "I have brought a gift from my mother, please take it and put them in some use, for anytime I see you, you are half naked"

Doctor Dale took the parcel from Britney with a smile of embarrassment on his face. Then Britney said in a cool voice "please open it" as she pulled a chair to sit down.

Doctor Dale opened the parcel and carefully examined the two white cotton t-shirt of his size at the back he recognized on one Britney's photograph then the other another elderly woman.

"Britney looked at Dale and said "that is me and the other is my mother"

Doctor Dale looked at his two guests with their gift in his hand then said "Please excuse me, I have clothes, I will put some on, by the way thanks for the gift" with these few words he open his little bedroom door to get some clothes on.

A few minutes later, he opened a bottle of Champaign, place it on the little table then placed three glasses and said "Welcome to my cabin for a drink"

As Doctor Dale poured his drinks of champagne he said "So miss Britney you never told me that your father is an English Army Captain"

Captain Hudson broke in "She told me about you encounter a few days back"

"I tried to save her life, but she was so proud of her beauty" said Doctor Dale.

"Of course! I am a young lady" said Britney with a smile on her pretty face.

"But if you die, your beauty will wither" said Doctor Dale.

"That is my dignity, handsome doctor" replied Britney.

"She is my only child, and when I met her mother she was a model, and the same way was her behavior, like a soldier always fight to conquer, even their lover, doctor" said Captain Hudson.

By the end of their drinks Britney and Doctor Dale became good friends, also some thing was common between the two of them.

Both of them hearts had a feeling for one another as a young couple.

All in all after a short while and a few drinks Captain Hudson leave with his pretty daughter Britney Hudson.

Chapter 4

A bu-Farouk Mohammed and his terrorist team were busy, some of his men who believed to be volunteers to helped the trapped in rubbles and below debris were just spies. They were spies in search for all types of prey to fall victim also for enemies of their organization, there were eyes on all the army camps especially the English and the American for they were their greatest enemies.

Eventually news got back to Abu-Farouk about Britney and her father Captain Hudson visits on the American warship, this seems to be of interest to Farouk. For it will be a feather to his crown, it was part of their mission, if in any way they could sabotage the American warship, thus his father would be proud of him. So his idea if he befriend pretty Britney he could persuade her to get on the warship at last if he step foot inside that ship that would be it for the American, for he is a scientist in building warheads for torpedoes.

Above all, he could sabotage any warplanes and misiles, but most of all if he could plant some bombs one wiring device in her then once safely on land, with a remote control in his hand as a child playing with a remote toy he will destroy that monster of a ship. That will cause the Americans and their parliamentarians to go crazy while his Muslim brothers laughing.

Abu-Farouk and his colleagues began to layout their plans, their first plan if some of their men could get onboard by helping the wounded into the Hospital the American provided in their warship, then their main idea was to anyone try for a break in what so ever means they came for the time was limited as for a few more days everyone will be leaving. Also withim few hours their full crew will set foot on this island and their main mission will be active.

Farouk at last decided as a play boy to have some fun with Britney, who will be of some great value to destroy their enemies, so he decided to travel down to Port-au-Prince with his expensive four wheel drive that they air lifted to this island.

Abu in his expensive jeep as a playboy, with his expensive clothing and a dark pair of glasses in a time like this it means many things like some Billionaires came here to donate a few million dollars to this badly in need island. Such was many celebrities and millionaires; such was journalists from various media groups.

All in all Haiti for the first time in its existence this poor island had attracted these kinds of people to walk on its soil, although in distress it was like a terrorist industry of movie making land, yet it was live a battlefield, it was such confusing as the rainbow and its colours of fantasy.

The sun was peeping from behind the high hills, easily showing itself to the people of Haiti beyond the herizon. However most of the people of this island had a hard night with their lights and the moon light to help in their rescue, but some hour everyone was glad for the rays of the lazy sun that was now peeping.

By this time the most handsome young man at present on this island Abu Farouk was strolling in his expensive four by four accompanied by his spy Fazeer Abdool who was a trained soldier as a pilot and nuclear weapons, down to a foot soldier also was a karate expert, these were the kind of men Abu-Sheriff Mohammed organization had brought for their job to be done.

They have spent Billions of dollars on their soldiers training. Therefore most of their men may exist for life, except for those suicide bombers they does not receive much training for they will have to commit suicide and money would be wasted.

These were the foolish that the organization fill their stomach with some thoughts of ill feelings and they held everyone as an enemy, given a few dollars to themselves also with the foolish beliefs that they will go to heaven where they will be paid for their rewards. It would be wealth, wives and other luxury for their foolish lives. But in the sight of the innocent these foolish individuals should not be given birth on this earth, yet Satan had created them.

Britney and her team were at work; they were on foot, Britney with the mike in her hand while Bill Samson with his camera on his shoulder, here Britney will pose herself to interview some one or to take out some pictures of ruins and casualties, then came Abu-Farouk with his cunning ideas.

"Hay, good morning Miss Britney Hudson, how you doing?" said Farouk with a wide smile.

At once Britney was interested in him for his handsomeness "Do I know you?" asked Britney.

"Yes, we met somewhere, I knew you. I am Doctor Vishall Gupta from India" said Farouk with his lying scheme trying to trap Britney in her remembrance.

"I find your face familiar" said Britney.

"Yes, as a Doctor I am usually doing research in my own field, also helping people who are in need." said Abu-Farouk.

"What can I do to help you sir?" asked Britney.

"Many things my friend" replied Abu.

"In what way?" asked Britney.

"Will you help me?" asked Abu-Farouk.

"If I can, I will definitely" replied Britney.

"Sure you can my charming friend" said Farouk.

Britney was looking into Farouk's handsome face with a pleasant smile whishing she could be his friend.

Abu-Farouk came out of his vehicle so that Britney could get a better look at him for he knew what he was capable of, he walked up to Britney and extended his hand in friendship, as Britney gave him a gentle hand shake, he held on to her hand looking down in to her eyes to hypnotize his opponent.

"I would like if you could come into the village of St. Mark and show the world what is taking place there as you had already done here" said Farouk.

"Well, I would be glad to but we do not have a vehicle to move about with" replied Britney.

"Well I have a few vehicles on this island. I could take you around, or if not of your desire, I could lend one to you for a few days" said Farouk.

"That's very kind of you" said Britney with a smile.

"Ok let's go to St. Mark and get some strange footage to show your people, I will bring you back" said Farouk.

Britney and her camera man Bill without hesitation took up a comfortable seat in Farouk four by four, this was their job to explore the island, but through to the urgentness there were no vehicle for them, so they were pleased if they could make their programme more efficient.

While in the four by four heading for St. Mark Farouk said directly to Britney, "You really can't remember me/"

"So much of Doctors I usually meet on errand" said Britney.

"I believe I met you in Afghanistan a few years ago" said Farouk to hear what Britney have to say.

"Only last night I met Mackintyre" said Britney.

"If he is handsome do you fall in love with him?" asked Farouk.

"He is interested in me and I had a little feelings for him to be truthful" answered Britney.

"I have met you the second time in my life and felt I could make you my children mother" said Farouk.

"Children mother? You said" belched Britney.

"I meant my wife" said Farouk with a chuckle.

"You are a handsome young man, you could find a wife at any time" said Britney.

"But not so pretty as you" replied Farouk.

"Well sir, please give it a little time" said Britney.

"Can we work on a project together?" asked Farouk.

"What kind of project?" asked Britney.

"You are a journalist and I am doing some research to further my studies, so I believe I could gain some help from you if we be good friends"

"As time progress we will see Doctor" said Britney.

By this time they arrived in St. Mark where Farouk had erected his camp for helping, together there were some other camps pitched scattered in the vicinity. There were some churches, volunteers and others doing what they can do to help.

In St. Mark everyone was busy just as in Port-Au-Prince, the situation was almost the same, but Britney landed in the village she began her walk. Her camera man Bill was busy while she was describing the situation of the surroundings and talking to casualties.

In the mean while Farouk had a chat with his colleagues so they began to call him sir, not his name again.

Britney was taken to be introduced to Doctor Fyzal Khan and others; she was impressed with their camp and the help towards the inhabitants. Britney and her camera man was introduced inside the camp. So they were allowed to take out photos of casualties to show the world the good things Abu organization was doing for the people of Hati. Cunning Abu did not posses the slightest idea, he was making a mistake, every one made mistakes. This casualty Mary Lucy Briggs caught the eyes of Britney and the camera.

Britney spent the whole day in St. Mark in the company of Farouk to develop his friendship to win her love. However his scheme was working for Britney was amazed of him and by the end of the day she was in love with him for he have all the necessities a pretty woman should look for, he was charming, had wealth, educated, there was nothing more a young lady would need to fall victim.

Chapter 5

Zabida Amena Mohammed, the Angel of Death, and the butterfly of love in the eyes of males was on her way with her expensive ship and team to be embarked to the island of Haiti within a few hours.

This Angel of Death, real name was "Zaman" she was born in Turkey, from Sheriff Mohammed off his fifth wife in Turkey. Her mother Zamela was the daughter of a wealthy businessman, there on business Sheriff Mohammed met her, with money and his Muslim influential power he bought her, then within a short while Zamela gave birth to Zabida. Zabida was born as a boy that consists of hormones as a male, however in his early teens, with money and and expensive surgery this child "Zaman" becomes a pretty young lady with the name of Zabida Amena.

The face and hormone surgery gave her the beauty, and then due to her education and job, she became the Angel of Death.

With millions spent on Zabida Education as an MD in Doctorate then to a scientist at PhD with other certificates in science and chemistry she becomes the Devil's wife. In her occupation she was an expert, her team was made up of other great scientists, they do not inherit their original sex, and they all went through the process of changed in their opposite sex.

In their occupation if they were suspected in any crime of terrorism they will immediately undergo the process of changing their features, they were the cruelest people that ever existed on the face of this universe. Their earnings for the year was a few Billion dollars, but they do not enjoy their earnings the organization utilized the money to finance terrorism.

Their business was selling of body parts to the wealthy millionaires through out the world, thus their contact was so large that they were finding difficulties to reach their demands. As a result they could be found operating in warfare countries, then to the poor countries.

In a warfare country they will act as a Red Cross unit to render assistance, in the process most patients or casualties went dead or missing, like the old and sick that they do not have use of any body parts. They will be treated and set free that everyone will witness, as for injured soldiers they will be put out of conscious then shipped to their head quarters where they were drugged for their used as suicide bombers they will be in their subconscious acting on Zabida's medication to carry out their mission, who were not fit for this circumstance, then good body organs were taken out for sale then their bodies were discarded.

As for ordinary citizens they were kidnapped, young boys and girls were trafficked in various market for sex, in this area they may change their sex and face in their operation as expert scientists to obtain a good price, some may also use for body organs as their market demand to supply, it all about money.

At times some victims who were no more fit for they bracket they were in, for the past few years, Zabida organization will buy them back at a cheaper price, put them to undergo a body change and resell some once again. Or if not they will be placed for body organs.

This Angel of Death and her expert team could store body parts for months in a re-fridgeration or built some mechanism to keep them alive for a few months.

At present this Angel of Death and her team will set foot on the soil of Haiti to render assistance as other had came on this island for.

This Angel of Death was two years senior her half brother Abu-Farouk, who was at present her lover in sex. They had met when their father Abu Sheriff had taken Zabida to see her smallest brother Farouk in Pakistan they were in their late teens. Zabida had spent a month in Pakistan at Farouk's mother home. At this time their love affairs began. Then as times goes by their father Abu Sheriff got information about the affair, hence he welcomes it with joy, for his half brother and sister they will make a good couple to serve his organization in a secret educational background.

At this point their father Sheriff Mohammed started his plan for them. However, Mr. Sheriff has a bundle of other children that was older, but yet he had foreseen a certain aspect that will solve many issues for him and his organization. With money was no financial problem, he decided to push their education to the fullest for his purpose then he began to groom them to become the Devil and the Angel of Death, here he groomed them in Afghanistan where civil war was on every day way of life. Then gradually they were being trained by highest terrorist group in Afghanistan, here their experienced growth and their habits of cruelty developed.

On the eve of the fourth day of Haiti devastation the Angel of Death's ship entered in the waters of Haiti, its name ""Allah Blessings"". It consists of a crew of fifteen under the Captain of Katija Ali. Katija Ali was born in Afghanistan as a boy, but his sex was changed at an early age, his real name was Kamal, his parents was a chief in command of organized terrorist group.

Thus from an early age his training began, then as a female she began her university Education in India. She then lived in Pakistan for some years as a key player in the terrorist organization then at last as she graduated in a highest degree in science with a PhD she was recruited by the Angel of Death for her life style was dirty with cruelty that was responsible for thousands of innocent lives.

At present she was a specialist in removing body organs, also she could implant any of the organs in an operation in a short while, because if the patient dies, his or her other organs goes on the market for sale. She was also expert in nuclear weapons also could maneuover any warplane of ships. Self defense and other miscellaneous training that an ordinary person will gladly achieve as their career.

Out of the fifteen scientists that made up the crew of the "Allah Blessings" at present eight were female while seven were male. Ironically all have been trained in various terrorist camps.

Their way of life, they have free sex with anyone of their crew partners as a cult member. Then comes the second in command of the Angel of Death crew member Doctor Rasheed Hamid whose name had changed to Waheeda. Rasheed born and grew up in Afghanistan. He then further his studies in a PhD degree in Indian. He was a medical Doctor and scientist. After his graduation in India he went back to Afghanistan to practice medicine, but his false scheme of making money among his country people of Muslims, he was sent directly to the terrorist group.

Rasheed as a male homosexual open his surgery but treated his patients with expired drugs and tablet that he obtained at a cheap price. But later on he killed most of his patients as he got a market from the trade of body parts so he was named "The Butcher"

Then later on as he fully joined the terrorist group with money in abundance in his hand he changed his sex and renamed himself as a female as Waheeda Hamid, but the name remained "The Butcher". However later on as she was recruited to Zabida crew she developed into a hater of human beings. Then to all these people, they will be sent to heaven at their death through Allah hu Ackbar to live in eternity in a world of paradise, this was their belief so no one could charge their cruelty.

Above all, this crew of humanitarians were coming to help these helpless people of Haiti.

The Angel of Death at last anchored her expensive and fully equipped ship "Allah Blessings" in the waters of Haiti, she was badly in need of help, but yet these scavenger came here, to feast, they brought food and medication to offer, however it was like a fisherman in the sea catching fishes for sale too maintain his livelihood. They will bait their hooks with some sort of fish or meat to catch a larger one for their profit.

The first of the crew to leave the large and expensive "Allah Blessing," that was anchored in the deep waters, were Zabida Mohammed followed by "The Butcher" Waheeda Hamid. They set afloat a small boat and from their ship to the beach, on the Caribbean island of Hati, from the beach, they walked on the shore of Haiti, a soil of great wealth for them, this was a fortune of wealth as they were ready and equipped, also the had their team led by Abu-Farouk Mohammed who had already sort out their way of taking their wealth secretly and confidently for the island was in a chaos.

Setting afoot on the soil of wealth for the "Angel of Death, they were greeted by their counterpart Abu-Farouk Mohammed and Doctor Faizal Khan to complete their mission as one team.

Zabida Mohammed engulfed Farouk Mohammed in closed arms to seal with a long lovers kiss so they could taste each other saliva, from this each once again after a long time could taste their love and read their distinguish plans in their own ways. At this point The Butcher joined Doctor Faizal Khan in their own conversation, for they all indulged in sex as a cult. This was their only way of relaxation in mating, and then the cruel things began to take shape in the formation of their work, but no fertilization of a new born terrorist. They will destroy the new born in their own womb, for it was their way of life.

After the long and sweet kiss Zabida said,

"In the name of Allah, is everything in place?"

"As usual! Nothing's a problem for us" said Farouk.

"Blessings be unto the almighty, Allah, for his faith in you is great, so we shall perform his duties" said Zabida.

"Peace be unto him, in his name his duties must be carried out" replied Farouk.

"That is why we joined you to perform and carry out the lord great Allah duties. So that we shall live in paradise with him" said Zabida.

"As I said peace be unto him, for through him we can all cooperate to complete our duties to him" said Farouk

"Do you have any cargo ready for our ship?" asked Zabida

"There are much as we wanted, we also have a choice of choosing, where we could select the best within a short while" replied Farouk.

"I do hope so, for we will take as much as we could for the ship is large and we come here equipped for business" said Zabida.

"Farouk looked at Doctor Faizal Khan and said in a low voice "Faizal, please tell my sweet heart how much wealth is waiting to be market!"

"There is a fortune to be taken within a few hours, in addition they are so many strong people, who are lots of casulties with no sickness in their body, this I personally examine. As such their cargoes will fetch a good market" said Faizal.

The Angel of Death looked at them and gave a broad smile of victory, then said "Peace be unto Allah, for he is great and so we shall do our duties, many of our colleagues are badly in need of these items what is at present wasting so let us make use of them, do not hesitate."

"We will immediately give our orders to get things in our way to make this precious occasion profitable" replied Farouk.

"Let us get started with haste" said The Butcher, doctor Waheeda Hamid.

The four of them without hesitation grouped in Farouk four by four then headed to their base to begin their dirty work for their God and people; for the innocent and helpless who need help, this was their luck and faith for their God had turned a blind eyes on them, while the others will gain because of their misfortune in life.

Chapter 6

In the year 2003 an American Army ship had anchored in the Caribbean Sea to the beach of Haiti. This Army ship was sent by the American Government to this poor island to gave medical assistance to the poor native inhabitants, this was a routine that the American Government usually gave aid to poor countries.

On board this Army ship was Doctor Ashton Benn at that time his rank was a Sergeant in his early thirties. Doctor Ashton was an American White with blonde hair and blue eyes as the Caribbean Sea. He was a huge man of an athletic build for a soldier. At that time he was very handsome as such any Caribbean young lady could fall victim to be a companion in his bed for comfort.

Mary Lucy Briggs a nurse from Haiti at that time was in her early twenties, pretty as a morning rose, she came from a Negro mother and a white father, thus a mixed race had showed their true colours in Mary. She had a pair of green eyes with black African hair, then the complexion of her white father, she was medium built but tall as the figure to be a top model to become a world beauty, proud Miss Mary Lucy as an educated nurse, she would break her style on other male and female nurses also some Doctors who were interested in her beauty. Also in her surrounding neighbourhood of a wealthy community, she was the one in all eyes.

Nevertheless there is a price for all priceless gems. Doctor Ashton Benn handsomeness and cunning smiles was the price for this gem as all strong and new ship will one day fall victim to the sea waves, but it matter of times, such as a pretty rose will wither and fall. Also as an apple or any fruits, then its seeds will one day rise into new plants as the seasons changes as the rain began to fall.

In that year 2003 Doctor Ashton met with pretty nurse Mary Lucy due to their profession, love once again began to bloom. It was like spring for these young lovers. They enjoyed the best of a love affairs, then as days goes by Doctor Ashton ship was ready to sail, such was the season changes to summer and the beauty of flowers and leaves will be seen among trees after atum.

As Doctor Ashton ship sailed away this pretty gem became pregnant as a fertilized seed was planted to be germinated. As the army ship sailed away over the waves of the Caribbean Sea to its destination, thus leaving the island of Haiti, hence like others that previously visited, then headed for another destination, so was Doctor Ashton brains and love, for the eyes will look for other beauties, as one was to eat a banana then throw the skin in the garbage. As hunger once again embraced will look for another orange to dine upon, leaving the skin to other in need of it like the rats and worms, but at the end of the day some one also could find a meal upon the waste discarded.

Pretty nurse Lucy got pregnant but her lover had sailed away beyond the horizon. Never could be found by her. At last she decided to develop the child in her womb. Then nine months later Lucy gave birth to a baby girl, she named her Stacy Ann.

Stacy inherited the looks mostly of a white race; her complexion was of a white, her eyes were blue as her father and grandfather but her hair was black and long, leaving its curly to show the inheritance of an African race. Surely she looked as a child's dolly, that captured the eyes of everyone as her mother had once.

As time rolled by Doctor Ashton Benn got the information that he had fathered a girl child in Haiti. But was not interested to find her, for this child was a mishap.

However Doctor Ashton remained in the American Army Doctor, but at present he was a major onboard the world's largest Army ship that thrown anchor in the waters of the Caribbean sea in Haiti at the present moment.

This island brought memories to him seven years ago, ironically his duties was to remain in the Army ship to help in the emergency of casualties that were taken on board, this was because he was a most senior and experienced Doctor to tend to patients in these circumstances.

Seven years ago he had a love affair on this island, but never in his thoughts he had any idea of looking for the daughter he had heard f or even seek to find the woman he once spent time in love.

However on February 12, 2010 this child Stacy-Ann like wise a few millions had the same experience as the earth had come to judgment day and that was the end to the planet of earth. Stacy-Ann at the age of six years old was playing with some other children in a day care home for children in Port-au-Prince, as the earth began to tremble, as usual everyone become nervous and frightened; as a result everyone was on their own to find their safety.

As everyone around the world had known as buildings began to crumble live body was trapped in collapsed buildings such was Stacy-Ann and her companions. Two days later rescue came to them, by this time some of her companions had gone to the lord, the maker as angels for they were innocent children.

There were rescue teams from all over the world working day and night non stop to save as much lives as possible. However as the American soldiers were busy as the bees likewise the ants working they came to the resque of these children. Stacy-Ann was unconscious, but as the soldiers who weas experienced in this kind of work place his hands on Stacy's body he realized her body was warm but not cold and rigid. So immediately he realized this child was alive. With haste she was taken to Doctor Dale Mackintyre attention.

Stacy Ann lying in front of Doctor Dale, she looked like a bed of a pretty flowers. At this age of six, her white inheritance could be seen distinguishingly, her still body of pettiness was like an angel as a sleeping rags, this Doctor Dale and his colleagues were accustomed to witness and signed their death certificates, with haste Dale began took to his work and prove how he got his certificate in Medicine. But he swore to himself he will not sign a death certificate for this child. He now brought her back to the civilization of planet earth. But yet again she was not the only casualties needed treatment, however she was special and should be given priority, may be this was her luck.

Ironically she was treated and put to rest in a special corner of the camp that Dale could have an eye on her for she was special to him.

Moments later the little angel came to life, with a squeak like a little rat feeding, it attracted Dale's attention, looking at her he saw that life was restoring in her. So at once she was given attention by Doctor Dale.

As the little angel came to life she was confused so she began to cry for mummy. Nevertheless she was cleaned and given new clothes. Then with some medication she was put once more to rest by Doctor Dale and so were others who were sent to this camp for first aid treatment.

Doctor Dale on seeing this little angel at first site, became interested in her, for he realized in this situation she should become an orphan as such he will be there to be the new father of this little angel.

That day of the ancident with this angel Dale did not see Britney Hudson for he was very busy, now this angel came in to his life that he admired, so he decided to work through the night, for the help of those helpless also to be there for this special infant.

The next morning came and Dale was tired and fatigued, he was badly in need of some rest, he was deciding what to do not wanting to loose this little angel. Then the pretty English journalist show up Britney Hudson.

"Good morning Doc, glad to see you in some clothes" said Britney with a smile.

Dale looked at her with a tired grin.

"Have any news to show to the world?" asked Britney.

"No news, but I have found an Angel, but … may God help me don't let our camera man have a glimpse at her!" replied Dale.

"Why?" asked Britney.

"Because I will choke him until these eye ball fall from its socket" replied Dale.

"Why is that so important" asked Britney.

"Just take a look at the treasure our boys found" said Dale pointing in a corner of the army camp where Stacy was sleeping.

Britney looked at the tiny body of a human being, then at Dale and walked to see what was so important.

Taking a good look at the child Britney whispered "Gosh, she is cute, really" then looked at Dale who was watching her with a side glimpse with the corner of his eyes.

Britney then touched her face gently, and then pass her fingers in her hair starting from her forehead as a comb of petting.

Stacy Ann woke up to see Britney in a dim vision. She held on to Britney's hand and cried in a soft tone "Mama … Mama"

Britney looked deeply into the child face then noticed her blue eyes. She then kneeled down on her knees, she then took the child to her breast, Britney then looked at Dale who was watching her "She have pretty blue eyes" whispered Britney.

"Don't! I said. Do not touch her" howled Dale.

"She needs her Mama" whispered Britney.

"She is an orphan" said Dale

"Then I will be her Mama" replied Britney.

"I am her new Pa-PA! I found her" said Dale directly to Britney with wide eyes.

"She is not an orphan as yet, further more no authority of law will give a child to a bachelor soldier boy" said Britney.

Dale walked up to Britney with his right hand on Britney wrist while his left hand on Stacy Ann shoulder trying to separate them and said directly with his two eyes wide open "Just get out of here immediately, you are disturbing my patient for her rest"

Britney realized what Dale was up to so in a cool voice Britney said "Doc, the child needs her mother ... and if you don't mind I will take her as her mama ... then as you said she is an orphan."

My gracious God Britney! Please leave as you came in my camp" said Dale as he put his pair of hands on his head.

"Please Dale I could take better care of her" said Britney with a friendly smile on her face.

"So I will become the looser; I brought her back to life" said Dale in a hoarse voice.

"That is your duty as a doctor, and my duty as a young lady duties is to be her mother" said Britney.

That statement sent Dale pressure to temper.

"Nurse please call a female soldier to get this British journalist out of my surgery please; I find she is disturbing my patient" shouted Dale.

While Stacy Ann yet clung to Britney moaning in a soft voice of tears "Mama, Mama"

Britney lifted Stacy Ann in her arms, with the child yet clinging to her, she then faced Dale and said in a soft voice "Doctor Dale, I know the both of us want this child, but if we behave foolish with haste we will both loose her, so please be reasonable, I will take care of her, then both of us will decide her fate, this I believe will be a hope for this pretty child's future"

Dale looked at Britney with defeat, then came to a reality that some how he will loose his treasure.

Then he said directly to Britney "Will you call her "Angel" that is her new name, promise me that"

"Yes! Her new name is Angel! Can I leave with her?" asked Britney.

Dale in tiredness looked at Britney and gave her a slow nod "Yes"

Without hesitation Britney Hudson left with Stacy Ann her new name "Angel".

Chapter 7

Nurse Mary Lucy Briggs had given birth to her daughter Stacy Ann and realized the miss fortune of love and reality of life. By this time she had owned an apartment of a small town house living in Port au Prince, but was working as a mid-wife in a nursing home in St. Mark, Haiti.

She maintained her beauty but never married. At present she had a lover who is an Engineer, who was born and bred in Haiti. His name was Paul Saxon. Paul was a lover of music as a result he was a key member of a musical band, but at the time of the earthquake he was in New York doing some music business he was a young man of some wealth he was handsome and honest. So he honestly worked his way to the position he earned in wealth. Lucy had received large sums of money from him at many times as such she owned her own home and living in some luxury. However Paul was not living home with Lucy but yet Paul was fond of Stacy Ann when ever he would spend a few nights by Lucy.

That morning on February 12, 2010 Mary Lucy had prepared for work living an ordinary life but kind of social, as she was leaving for work she would drive Stacy to school, then to her work place, then in the evening a special taxi would take Stacy after school to a day-care center. Then in the evening as Lucy will be returned from work she would stop by the day care to take up Stacy and then headed for home, however that evening she never made it to Stacy day care centre.

That evening as Mary Lucy was preparing to leave the Hospital, a short while before she could leave as usual, all at a sudden Haiti was trembling and so was the people of this native land. Haiti was vibrating so hard that the buildings could not up keep their strength. The weak were falling one by one, then there were the echoes of screams of human from every where, it was the cries of defeat.

At this moment a few million people suffered in many ways, man, woman and helpless children. Many were buried alive while others were pinned below debris suffering in pain for days, in this island at present everyone needed help.

Mary Lucy work place had crumbled like the other buildings; no one could help one another. Some were dead while some were conscious, what a dreadful nightmare. It was like a horrible dream, that anyone who was experiencing a dream like this was glad to be awaken, but everyone lives was in the hands of the almighty.

But the almighty God know his work. Some may say that they are unfortunate, however in God's hands everything is skillfully drafted out for he never made mistake, he will bring pains and sufferings then at last the tidings of good.

After the collapse of Lucy work building and everyone was trapped inside, some long hours passed by then they were rescued. Unfortunately they were rescued by the wrong group of rescuers. They were Abu Farouk Mohammed's men that came to their aid; this was by the day before the Angel of Death arrived.

That was the day Britney had visited Abu Farouk camp. Lucy and some others casualties were treated by Doctor Fyzal Khan and Abu had put some of them to rest in an unconscious state for their own purpose because the ship "Allah Blessings" will soon be arrived and these will be some of its cargoes.

However as Britney and her cameraman together with her full crew had visited Abu Farouk camp they had taken out photographs of these victims, but what caught Britney eyes was this pretty middle aged lady Lucy's body. To Britney the body looks to her as somebody in a position according of its features also as a mixed race; it was not in a ragged condition of other Negroes of Haitians birth.

Then by seeing this child Angel her memories came upon this unknown Lucy, within all the dead and casualties she had seen within these past hours, these two figures caught her eyes. It was some thing of instinct or by they were of a mixed breed of some whites. Above all it was in the memory of Britney's imagination.

"Angel" Stacy Ann was in the companion of Britney, that evening as Britney tried to comfort Angel it did not take them too long to become friends. Britney question her about her whereabouts, at last Britney learnt that angel real name was Stacy Ann Briggs, her mother name was Mary Lucy Briggs and that she was a mid wife in Nursing Home working in St. Mark. For at this time Stacy Ann was twelve years old and was quite talkative yet friendly. About her father Britney learnt that her father was in Europe and her uncle name was Paul Saxon who played music, but was not living home with her mother.

At once this brought back the memories at St. Mark in Abu Farouk camp so she got all the pictures from her camera man Bill Samson. Britney showed Stacy Ann all sort of photos but as Britney showed her the mixed female photographs, Angel pointed at it saying "Mama … Mama".

Hence Britney realized her instinct was leading to the right path. Britney decided to use her intelligence for the needed to help this child find her mama. But do not want to carry this child to identify her mother in both states of conditions, so she decided to give her back to Doctor Dale who loved her so much too. Also she would be comfortable with him. Britney asked Stacy Ann "Do you want to see your real papa"

"Yes!" replied Stacy Ann.

"If you see him would you recognize him?" asked Britney.

Stay Ann shook her head sideways with a sad face.

"Ho Ho. I will take you to daddy" said Britney.

"Not Daddy! Papa" said Stacy Ann.

"OK will you stay with papa?" asked Britney.

Stacy Ann gave a slow nod of "Yes" with a little smile then asked "Where is mama?"

"I am going to find you mama" answered Britney.

"You promise" Britney gave her a nod of yes, then a smile and said "yes"

"OK then I will stay with papa until mama came to take me home" said Stacy Ann.

Britney gave Stacy a kiss and said "Good Child"

"You are mama's friend?" Stacy asked.

"No! But I know where to find her" replied Britney.

"So find her for me please" said Stacy Ann

"We will be on our way right now" replied Britney.

"You have any baby, I will play with them" said Stacy.

Britney gave Stacy a broad smile and said "No honey"

"OK then take me to papa" said Stacy Ann.

Britney took Stacy's arms as they walk down a short distance to Doctor Dale camp.

As Britney and Stacy enter Doctor Dale surgery he was already early and busy in his job, as the two females walked up to Dale, Britney pointing to Dale said to Stacy Ann "Look! He is your papa"

''No He isn't my papa! Replied Stacy.

''Yes, he is; he sailed away with a boat, so he come back.'' Said Britney smiling at Dale.

Ok I will go and ask him." Replied Stacy.

Dale looked in astonishment as Stacy Ann walked towards him saying "Papa"

Dale looked at Britney who gave him a wide smile then she said "I have brought back your treasure, take care of her" then she walked out of Dale's camp to compete her promise.

Dale open his two arms in front of him in a welcome manner as Stacy Ann walked in to him in a hug humming the words "Papa" Dale responded to Stacy by saying "will you stay with papa?"

"Yes" she said "you is my papa" reply Stacy.

Stacy continued her statement saying, as she pointed to Britney. "She is going to find mama"

"She knows your mama?" asked Dale.

"Yes! She told me she know my mama and she is going to find her" replied Stacy

"Well if she don't find your mama, will you stay with papa?" asked Dale.

"She had one of mama photographs, she showed it to me and I told her that is my mama" said Stacy.

Dale looked at the child then scratched his head "What is going on" he said to himself.

"Papa; my mama said, my papa is a doctor, Is you the Doctor who sailed away on a ship" said Stacy.

"Your mama said you papa is a doctor who sailed on a ship?" asked Dale in confusion.

"Yes my mama said my papa is a white soldier Doctor who sailed away on your ship"

said Stacy. In confusion Dale repeat in a whispered "your papa is a soldier doctor who sailed way on his ship?"

Looking at the child she has white inheritance. "Then who is this Army Doctor Child" Dale asked himself.

Dale then looked into Stacy eyes and asked her "Does your mama ever told you your father name?"

"Yes, his name is Doctor Benn. Is your name Doctor Benn?" asked Stacy Ann.

Dale slowly shook his head with a nod, as his pair of his eyes looking a this pretty and talkative child, then said softly to Stacy "Call me papa, that's all"

Doctor Dale an educated soldier boy realized what went wrong for this child birth, some white soldier is the father of this child, they spent their happy times with this child mother then sailed away, but by the way who is the Doctor Benn?

Doctor Dale put all these ideas behind his back, placed Stacy in a comfortable place to past her day and began to tend to his work for the morning was early and casualties were beginning to line up for the Doctors yet there were a team of Doctors working but yet their work was heavy because of the millions of people that had been suffered.

Doctor Dale Macintyre began to think, he fell in love with this little angel that he wanted to adopted, to his conscious he might be a soldier for the rest of his life then in his old age he may want a child as his comfort to be proud someday; the again this child father is a white army doctor.

In addition Britney Hudson knew the mother of this child, what is going on, yesterday she wanted this child so badly that by force she took her away, then this morning she brought back the child, telling her that I am her doctor father who was a soldier on this island. After that, she leave to find the child's mother in his densely devastated island, also the child claims that Britney show her, her mother photograph. What a broken puzzle for Doctor Dale to fix just because of this innocent child.

Chapter 8

The "Angel of Death", Zabida Mohammed, the cannibal touch down in St. Mark, Haiti. Seeing the priceless gem worth money, without any hesitation her communication system began to work as she owned a satellite for her network in her business.

Zabida seeing young and pretty Mary Lucy, she said "Take her onboard alive, she herself is a fortune"

"Organs or Life?" asked Abu Farouk

"So much organs dying and wasting, why kill her, she should be sold as a stripper or some black Muslim with millions will pay good for her, she will keep them comfortable in bed" answered Zabida.

"So what your cargo will consist of?" asked Farouk

"Heavenly children, male and female, to be sold" answered Zabida.

"Then what about the casualties?" asked Farouk

"The casualties should be butchered, that is why I brought The Butcher on land, to do his work" said Zabida.

"When we begin to load your vessel?" asked Farouk

"As it most suitable for you, you were here before me, so you know better" said Zabida.

"OK during the night it is safe, for the entire island is in darkness, then no one will not realized what is going on, expect us, everyone will be busy in their own way of help" said Farouk

"Let tonight be the big operation" said Zabida.

"We will make hay while the sun shines" said Farouk

"Do you already have an organization functioning?" asked Zabida.

"Just some food stuff and water to drink is all their payment" said Farouk

"Do you have trust in these native people?" asked Zabida.

"We have already organized a group of them, they will dig in the rubbles or take any one from the street that suits us, then at last they could be on the ship easily as slaves, so we carry our secrets with us; there is nothing to worry about, peace be unto Allah" belched Farouk.

As the sun hid itself beyond the high hills, then slide beyond the horizon, the island of Haiti become dark. Then the glare of headlights could be seen like candle flies performing their duties, so was Farouk men. The road that was in communication these men knew well, there was no police to controlled traffic, because there was no law at present on this island, everyone's business was free. So the crew of "Allah Blessings" will have an easy task ahead tonight to load its cargo of human and their organs.

Mary Lucy and some others were the first batch to be transported on "Allah Blessings".

That night was a second nightmare for some people in Haiti. The Butcher began to rip off hearts, liver, kidneys and other internal organs. Their bodies were dumped or buried by some well paid natives, as was already organosed, for the little they would received as money, clothes, foodstuff or water that was a fortune for them, but yet they were betraying their own country in greed for themselves to survive as was done in Africa on the slave trade during the16th and 17th century.

The first night was a busy and profitable one. Yet during the coming day they will also be busy stocking up casualties in their camps to begin an early work as the darkness gathered.

It was about half eight in the morning Britney and her team showed up at Abu Farouk camp known to her as Doctor Vishal Gupta. Abu Farouk together with Zabida and their colleagues had a hectic night; the camp was bloody from the work of The Butcher and others not using enough drugs in their work of operation. So the camp smelled fresh with these human blood.

Appearing at the camp Britney was greeted by Doctor Vishal Gupta (Farouk)

"Good morning Doc" said Britney.

"Good morning my pleasant friend" answered Farouk.

Britney looked at Farouk and could see the tiredness in his face, with a smile on her face she said "Like you hard a hard night?"

"May God bless the rescue workers. Works so willingly and whole heartedly for these people that we have treated a great amount of casualties as you could see the condition of the camp" said Doctor Gupta (Farouk)

"After treatment where are they?" asked Britney.

"As you see our camp is so small to accommodate many casualties as a hospital, so we treated them accordingly then we sent them to other shelter where they could get some rest in a nearby shelter and food. There is nothing more we can do for we gave as much help as we could" answered Farouk.

As Britney was having the morning conversation with Farouk, Zabida showed up from one of the room as a butcher shop, she had on her gown; it was kind of bloody for her pretty face and feminine figure. Britney looked at her in envy, for she was pretty for a doctor.

Without hesitation smart Abu said "Britney meet my sister Zabida, Zabida this is Britney Hudson from the BBC news network in England, and she calls me Vishal"

The three of them looked at one another for Zabida got the message Farouk name was Vishal. Zabida quickly pull the sanitary gloves off her hands and gave Britney a brief handshake then said "Please to meet you Britney, it is a pleasure meeting people like you all over the world"

"Thanks doctors for the help that you all render to these helpless people all over the world, may God bless you, as for me I could only show the world the good things that you are doing in a situation like this" said Britney.

Zabida then looked at Britney for her appearance this morning was un-welcomed so as she turn to go she said "Sorry to excuse you, but I have work to tend to that is important"

"That's fine" said Britney to Zabida with a smile.

As Zabida evacuated the company of Farouk and Britney Farouk asked "Is there any thing I could do for you?"

"Just a small favour!" replied Britney.

"Yes, please ask me any favour once it is in my line I will humbly do it for you" answered Farouk.

"OK yesterday morning as you were showing me around I saw a Mullato woman in your camp, I need to see her." said Britney.

Abu Farouk faced looked puzzled for he knew who Britney is asking for, but he was so cunning he replied

"To be honest, so much of casualties are being treated in this camp then leave, I can't remember none of them"

"OK then if I show you a photograph of her, could you recollect some idea of her?" asked Britney.

Professor Farouk looked more confused but trying to fixed his face as if he is thinking about the Mulato that Britney is asking for, in his brains he was thinking if something went wrong and a leak got to the media, why Britney came here specially to see this special woman, whom they cannot give account for to the law.

Farouk looked directly into Britney's eyes then asked "Is there any problems with her, why she so special?"

"At present you have to help me find her, for I promised her little daughter I will find her mother" replied Britney.

"How do you know she have a daughter and that exact woman was treated in this medical camp?" asked Farouk.

Britney took out the photograph of Lucy lying on a bed, the photograph was about eleven inches by seven inches, then handed it to Farouk as she said "I took these photographs yesterday as you were showing me around then in the evening we found her daughter, this photograph I ran form the camera to my computer then to my printer and this what I could make out of her, then the child recognized her mother"

In a puzzled brain Farouk took the photograph, looked at it carefully for at present was fully aware about this woman then he said to Britney "Excuse me please I will take this photograph inside and find out if I could get some help for you, however I would not promise you that anyone would recognize her.

Farouk walked inside the camp leaving Britney outside, he then went and discussed the problem with the Angel of Death Zabida.

Zabida looked at the photograph then at Farouk, listened to what he had to say, and then said "Let me handle this."

Zabida revisited Britney with a cunning smile she said directly to Britney "Why taking all this headache when we could handle this so easily"

"What do you mean?" asked Britney.

"Leave the photograph with us; we will try to investigate where she went, in the mean time you could bring the child here so you would not have any problem"

Britney paused to think.

Then Zabida continued "You have the work of the media to do, so we as well have the wellfare to give these people medication for a new life, that is all what we all came here for"

"I promised that child, I will find her mother" said Britney

With a big smile on Zabida pretty face she said "That child must be pretty according to her mother photograph?"

"She is cute" replied Britney.

"OK let us handle that minor problem for you, get the child down here as fast as possible so that we could help you locate the mother and if the mother can't be found I will adopt the child as my own, once she is cute as you said" said the Angel of Death.

"She has already found a Doctor as her father, who is willing to adopt her" said Britney.

"Well why worry miss, go about your work the child is so lucky that she found a Doctor as her father, her mother can't brought her up to be like an adopted Doctor Father" said Zabida.

Britney looked at Zabida then said in scorn.

"Her real father is a white soldier Doctor"

"Whooo! She must be really cute, and then I could offered to be her adopted mother who will take more care of her" said Zabida.

Imagine if she got hold of this child how much money she could make or what she could make out of her in future to carry her job.

"OK Doc give me the photograph as I will be doing my job I will inquire if any one knows her whereabouts" said Zabida stretching her hand to give back Britney the photograph of Mary Lucy.

Zabida handing Britney's back her photograph, said "Have a good day and make sure you show the photograph of the world the good things our organization is doing to help these people of Haiti"

Britney took her photograph of Mary Lucy, looked at it carefully then asked herself "Where could this woman have gone, only yesterday she saw her lying unconscious on one of these bed in this said camp, where the hell is she, then her promise to the child."

As she walked towards the cameraman Bill Samson who was busy taking all types of photographs, she began to discuss the problem with him trying to get some answers.

Bill Samson with his big belly and bald head like a pumpkin sitting on a stool peered over his glasses to look at Britney pretty face and said "We will find her; we will show the photograph to the people around some one must see her"

''But Bill, where could the woman disappear, that is a mystery, nobody knows anything about her, if she wasn't there we should not have gotten her photograph" belched Britney to Bill.

"Be patient we will find her, you promised the child you will find her mama, but not today, we have more time, but definitely we will find her" said Bill.

So they go about their business Britney was showing the people of the area finding out if they have any idea of her. But a few answers were that they know her as a midwife in the hospital, but after the earthquake they never saw her.

Some answered were they never know her, yet Britney continued showing the photograph to villagers to find about her whereabouts.

Chapter 9

The island of Haiti becomes so popular in the world wide internet and broadcast, the news of an earthquake victims, everyone was looking on their television set for its news cast, as everyone was asking for a donation to be utilized in this island.

However as the foreigners with money were willing to help in some way, so were the people of Haiti who migrated from this island and found betterment. They too were willing to help in some way for it is the country of their birth was suffering.

However, Paul Saxon, Mary Lucy present lover decided to cut his business trip short and travel back to Haiti to seek his loved ones and render any assistance as possible. He told himself they may be weak or fall victim to casualties as such a healthy and strong man it means many things.

At last Paul Saxon was in Haiti, his home after a short while of the sad earthquake and his ruined homeland, at once he began his mission to look for his loved ones, some close ones could be found as they were looking for the other relatives. But there were no account of his lover Mary Lucy or Stacy Ann. To his calculation at the time of the earthquake Lucy should be at work or in the vicinity of St. Mark, so with no answers from Port-au-Prince he decided to seek help in St. Mark.

On his arrival of the little town of St. Mark, the first thing he did was to check with the Hospital that Lucy was working at. But to his eyes looking for the building, he realized it had crumbled. He decided to go through the debris, but there was no life. It could be seen that some rescue team had combed the demolished buildings for bodies.

He then turned to all the Red Cross or any medical camp any way of means needed people may seek help. But there was no Lucy. With a photograph in his wallet of Mary Lucy and Stacy Ann he began to show the villagers for any information to seek help.

Britney Hudson and her team were doing well covering the scene of Haiti and the happening with all activities so the world at large could see, some may offer money or donate some items useful, while some may offer prayers, but something was offered to these people, however they must receive a little of something if no water, food or medication may be a little God's help.

Britney's day was about to end, in her job she was prosperous, but her promised to this little child had failed, what will she tell this child?

With the hot sun of the Caribbean and a hard day's work Britney and her team were tired, so by evening they decided to get some rest, so may be during the late in the night, they may have to some footage if any situation arises, but Britney does not make her way straight to their camp. She went in search of Stacy Ann and Doctor Dale for her own reasons. One idea was to plea to Stacy Ann for a next day then to see if Dale needed any help with the child.

On her arrival at Dale's camp Stacy was comfortable with the nurses playing in their cabin, but at Britney presence Stacy Ann becomes worried.

"Miss Britney you find mama? You sure did promise me that!" said Stacy Ann

Everyone was looking at her with sympathy for she was not the only child with this fate at present, there were hundreds of thousands facing the similar situation, yet she was lucky because of her beauty.

Britney with sympathy said "Please honey give me one day more; tomorrow for sure!"

"But I want my mama, I want to go home" said Stacy

"All the homes are destroyed" answered Britney.

"Angel, you promised you will stay with pap' butt in Dale.

"I promised I will be with you in the day" said Stacy.

"OK you will sleep with me tonight once more" said Britney.

"If I have no choice I will stay with you tonight, but you promised you will find my mama" said Stacy.

Dale looked at Britney with a puzzled face, and then said "I knew I will be hard on you to find her mama, but you said you know where to find her, what happened?"

"It was not how I expected it to be so easily, from yesterday morning to this morning, there is a vast difference in time in a situation this island position is at present" answered Britney.

"You have her photograph, then you saw her in a medical camp, where could she be?" asked Dale.

"That is a puzzle for me right now" said Britney.

"Much difficult! What should we do from here?" asked Dale.

"She just disappeared" said Britney.

"Well it's a mystery for you to solve as a journalist" said Dale.

"OK let's work out some thing for her, she will be with me tonight then tomorrow I will drop her back right here, then I will try again" said Britney.

"Then at the end you will be the next mother, that is no problem for me, take care of her, nevertheless I will be there for her at any time of difficulties" said Dale.

"She is a child of high birth, she is smart and I fully know most millionaire couples will gladly accept her if she goes on the adoption board" said Britney.

"Fine let us do our own duty and we shall be the first to be on the adoption list" said Dale.

"Doc, let us not cause a feud over this child within a few more days we will all have to leave this island, then she will have to be on her own, after that there will be nothing we could do for her" said Britney.

"I am agreed with your Britney, but she is quite personally, I will like to make her my child, but God knows the best for her life." said Dale.

"Her father is an army doctor and so is you some soldier had abandoned her mother, then another soldier doctor wanted the child" said Britney.

"Maybe the father does not know what he had abandoned" said Dale.

"That is the work of all soldiers in foreign land, in their youth young girls is their desire then gone about their business" said Britney.

Dale began to think then said "I know of a Benn, Aston an Army Doctor onboard my ship who is a crew member, I will have a chat with him, may be he could tell me something" Said Dale.

"Ok to help this child you work on that, while I will try once again to find the mother" said Britney.

Britney held Stacy Ann to leave, as she was leaving with Britney. She was waving her tiny hand saying "goodbye papa. I will see you tomorrow again."

"Yes, you will be by papa tomorrow, sleep with Miss Britney" said Dale with a smile.

"You too papa" shouted Stacy.

'' See you in the morning, honey.'' Whispered Dale to Stacy.

"Thank you papa" said Stacy Ann.

"And don't give any trouble" replied Dale.

"No papa" shouted back Stacy Ann.

Britney was smiling as she move away with little and pretty Stacy Ann as they were walking away she would turn back regularly to look at the army camp.

At this point Britney could feel her heart go out for her, then her infant days with her mother and father.

That evening Britney took Stacy Ann to meet her father Captain Anderson Hudson of the British navy, who also had a hard day for everyone was busy because of lives to be saved then the island was in a mutiny for the survival for water and food.

That was late in the evening, Captain Anderson was having a meal and same time to rest then to pass his orders, in a time like this some one in command had to make good decisions or else they will have to answer to higher Authority when the mission is completed.

Britney entered her father little office where he gave his orders, Stacy Ann was by her side.

"Good evening Captain" greeted Britney.

"Same to you my child" answered Captain Anderson,

then said "like you found a companion?"

"Doctor Dale found her" replied Britney.

"I guess by now she is an orphan" said Anderson.

"As you will say Dad because of the situation of this island" replied Britney.

"Oh yes! There are thousands of them right now in all the camps that we pitched up for shelter, may God have mercy upon them" said Anderson.

"Dad have a good look at her, she is an exceptional!" replied Britney.

"Yes! What I can see is she is three quarters of white" belched Captain Anderson.

"Yes! That is what I can see too, but she claimed her father is a white doctor soldier who sailed away leaving her mother" said Britney.

The Captain Shook his head sideways then gave a steupes and said "it always happens, I met your mother in Punjab, there I was based in India at that time she was as beautiful as you, but I made her my wife which is your mother if I had abandoned her, you would have been in the same position as her my child, however all soldiers from the navy is not the same" said Captain Anderson.

"Oh dad I always love you and mom" said Britney.

"Your mother was always a good Punjabi woman until I brought her to England where you were born" replied Captain Anderson.

Stacy Ann was looking at Captain Anderson quietly "look at her eyes, it is blue as the sky, it is perhaps her fathers' just like you, you have your father eyes, they too are blue" said Anderson.

"Dad the reason I brought here is because I have a promise her to find her mom" said Britney.

"What foolish promise you have made to this child, in a position like this, look at the condition of this island, where on heaven can you find her mother" said Captain Anderson.

"Dad yesterday morning I have seen her mother in a refugee camp in St. Mark, then this morning I went back to find her, however there is no clue of her" said Britney as she handed her father the photograph of Mary Lucy.

Captain Anderson took a good look at the photograph then raised his head to look once more directly at Stacy ann. "this woman is a Mulato, she too came from some white background" he said.

"Dad, by chance do ever notice anyone look like her?" asked Britney.

"Please leave this with me, I will show it to the soldiers if they ever come across someone familiar to her." said Captain Anderson.

At this time Stacy Ann broke her silence" will you find my mama, please"

Both Britney and her father looked at one another in a sad smile then looked at Stacy Ann.

"I will try to, but I am not promising you that my sweet heart" said Captain Anderson in a low voice.

"I want my mamma, I want to go home" said Stacy Ann.

"Does your mama ever teach you to pray?" asked Anderson.

"Yes, I could pray" as she began top pray "Our father who art in heaven, please hear my prayer ... as she continued to pray. At the end Captain Anderson said "then God will help you, he is in heaven and he heard every one prayer, so if you continued praying you will find your mama"

"Then I will promise you I will pray to find my mama!" said Stacy Ann.

But I will not promise you I will find you mamma all I will try to help but in your prayers God will promise you that" said Captain Anderson.

"But Miss Britney promise me by tomorrow she will find my mama" replied Stacy Ann.

"OK honey stick to God and miss Britney and they will help you find your mamma" said Captain Anderson"

"Thank you sir" answered Stacy Ann.

After a short meeting with Britney and her father she explained every thought she knew about the child.

They both decided to help in some way, Britney then went and took to her rest for the next day's work.

Chapter 10

Paul Saxon was searching the village of St. Mark fir his lover Mary Lucy, he was looking furiously, with desperation, with the photograph he got some answers, but the answer was no help, yet it could lead to some opening, he was famous in the island because of his career in the music business, once heard his name anyone will try to think and help.

The answer he got was a young white journalist was also looking for her with a photograph, the same likeness and name.

Depressed Mr. Paul Saxon went from refugee camp to all the medical centers in St. Mark. He also visited Abu Farouk medical camp, their answer was also no. however this sent a message to Abu Farouk and Zabida, was she so important? Why? Never the less for these terrorist they had her secured in their ship "Allah Blessing", she was in a cage to the bottom level. In this ship's dungeons, where the engine room is situated. It is made up of small cages to hold captives alive; such was Mary Lucy and others in Haiti.

The next night of their operation for these terrorists their movements was slow for they have to be more careful. The Butcher worked became lesser for that night, they had decided to secured more life casualties rather than body organs, their thoughts was to work fast, but must have enough value as cargoes to reach their demand then sailed away before any suspicion arose, they will claim that their food and medication ran out and that was why they were leaving.

Doctor Dale Mackintyre of the US navy kept his promise once onboard his ship that evening tried to get in touch with Doctor Ashton Benn who rank was at present Captain Ashton.

Dale had found Captain Ashton in his cabin late that night; for he too was busy in the intensive care unit onboard their ship.

As Dale entered Captain Ashton's cabin, he was busy with some x-rays.

"Good night Captain" as a greeting from Doctor Dale.

"Good night Doc, glad to see you; everything OK?" asked Captain Ashton.

"Yes, but just want to share some of your time" answered Dale.

"Is there a problem" as the Captain Ashton looked Dale in his eyes reading them.

"No Captain just a formal conversation" said Dale.

"Make yourself comfortable" replied Ashton.

Dale made himself comfortable in a chair facing Captain Ashton Benn.

"Need some coffee or whisky?" asked Captain Ashton.

"Thank you I will take both, whiskey in the coffee, if you don't mind" said Dale.

"That is fine you are welcome" said Captain Ashton as he made a drink of whisky for himself then some coffee as he was throwing the whisky in the coffee cup he said "Strong"

Dale looked at him with a grin and said "that will be fine for me, the day was so hectic"

"For all of us soldier boy, this earthquake had made a history on this island, by the way what brought you here, if you don't mind" said Captain as he handed Dale his coffee then take a seat.

Dale took a good drink then looked at Captain Ashton face slowly he began "Captain about seven years ago, by some how you were present on this island?"

Captain Ashton face changed at this question, wanting to know why this question was raised.

"Is that a question on the line of duty!?" asked Captain Ashton.

"No just formal and friendly" said Dale.

"What is it you want to know?" asked Captain Ashton.

Dale looked at the Captain Ashton face worried and anxious to hear what he had to say.

"There is a little girl by the name of Stacy Ann, she is mixed with white and maybe mulatto, she have blue eyes as a white man, she claimed her father is an Army Doctor" said Dale.

Captain Ashton smiled and sat back in his chair comfortable, then said "yes, seven years back I was on this island rendering medical assistance."

"Do you on that time had an affair with any young girl at that time" asked Dale.

"That is my personal soldier boy, but I will tell you yes my boy" said Captain Ashton.

"So this child was right, her father is an army Doctor by the name of Benn?" asked Dale.

"Doctor Dale what are you telling me, that you have encountered a child claiming I am her father?" asked Captain Ashton.

"To be honest Captain that is the truth" said Dale.

"Oh my God, I have a child on this island? Oh sweet Mary Lucy where are you?" said Captain Ashton.

"So you remember Mary Lucy? What she looked like Captain?" asked Dale.

"She is soft as my blanket and sweet as the whisky. She is African mixed with white with blue eyes, but I couldn't not make her my wife for she was a coloured, but yet she kept me comfortable in bed until our ship finish its time and we sailed away" said Captain Ashton Benn.

"Captain if so be the case, your child became an orphan, we found the child but her mother went missing" said Dale.

"What is the child look like?" asked Captain Ashton.

"She is about five or six years old, so qute and sweet that I could make her my own child" said Dale.

"Really? Soldier boy? asked Captain Ashton.

"Captain, come to reality they are suffering out there, they are human beings, they need help and you are the one should put some emphasis on this for the sins you have created" said Dale.

"OK tell me something about them?" asked Captain Ashton.

"That is why I am here for you to tell me something about the mother Mary Lucy" said Dale.

"Doc I told you about Lucy, and then you told me about the child, what more do you want to know about my life in Haiti this ruined island" replied Captain Ashton.

"Lord have mercy, I am trying to help a child that claims you are her father, I need help to find this child's mother to unite them in love, if you don't need love, this child needs it" said Dale.

"OK Doc will you do me a favour, bring the child to me, if she prove to be mine under a blood test I will take care of her, but the truth is, that after we sailed away I never heard anything from her, believe me Doc, honestly" said Captain Ashton.

"OK Captain I will bring that child onboard with your permission and if the child is yours promise me she will legally be my daughter on the adoption board, I will take care of her under the law" said Dale.

"As you wish Doc, I am willing to help, poor soldier boy, need a help or something, I will do you that favour if it is in my power" said Ashton.

Dale got out of his chair and looked at Captain in his face and said "promise" and walked out of Benn's Cabin.

The next day bright and early miss Britney Hudson set to full fill her promise to this orphan child, she took Stacy to Doctor Dale camp of casualties and medication, Dale explain his meeting with Captain Ashton Benn to Britney, however, Stacy was left behind with Doctor Dale as the previous day.

Once again Britney and her cameraman were in St. Mark with a next copy of Mary Lucy's Photograph.

So was broken hearted Mr. Paul Saxon, Paul was with the idea of looking for this young English journalist to find out the reason why she too was looking for his lover Lucy.

Paul sighted the pretty journalist as he was looking for in the street of St. Mark, she had a photo in her hand showing to passersby.

"Good morning miss" said Paul to Britney.

She looked at Paul and said "Hi" with a smile.

"Please miss let me see that photograph you have in your hand, I do believe I could give some help" said Paul politely to Britney.

Britney handed Paul the photo, he then looked at the photograph of his lover Mary Lucy, the photograph showed Lucy was lying on a small bed with her eyes closed, his eyes watered as it fell on Lucy's photo.

Britney saw the emotion, at once she knew she had brake a code to open a chest of wealth and her promise will fulfill to this child

"You know her"?" asked Britney.

"Yes1, she is my lover, I am searching for her everywhere" said Paul with a sad face.

"Do you find any clue of her?" asked Britney.

"Where you got this photograph from" asked Paul

Britney looked at Paul sad face, pointing to Farouk's medical camp she said "I visited that medical camp the day before yesterday and there she was so my cameraman took a few footage, so she happens to be there"

"I heard you were looking for her yesterday" replied Paul"

"Yes!" said Britney.

"So was I" replied Paul.

"Do you find anything" asked Britney.

"All I know was that you were looking for her too, so I decided to find you so here I am, that is all I know about her whereabouts" said Paul.

OK so the two of us are looking for the said missing person" said Britney.

Paul took out his wallet open it and handed it to Britney.

Britney took the wallet and look at the photograph what she saw, pretty Mary Lucy in full beauty holding little Stacy Ann she then looked at Paul in his face with a full glance.

"This means anything to you?" asked Paul.

"It make much sense to me, her child, this little girl at present is in my possession, that is the reason I am looking for her mother, this I promised her I will find her mother" said Britney.

Oh thank you please, at least I have found Stacy, I will take care of her until I find her mother" said Paul with a little relief on his face.

Britney studied Paul face then think of Dale and said "you could see her, but you can't take custody over her until later" said Britney.

"That is fine with me, for sure she will not be an orphan to strangers, I will take care of her, I am very fond of her, but her mother is the problem for now" said Paul.

"Do you have any idea where we could find her?" asked Britney.

"Let us start back from the medical camp, where you last see her" said Paul.

"Glad to meet you, my name is Britney Hudson from the media of BBC. Look around, if you find anything please get in contact with me, as you know I have my work to do. If you want to see Stacy you are free to." said Britney.

"Miss Britney please do me a favour, let us go back to that medical camp where you took out this photograph, because personally I went and enquire there and they turn me down with a "no" to all my questions." said Paul.

"I will do you that for you, Doctor Vishal Gupta is a friend of mine, may be he could recall and give us some clue" said Britney as they began to walk towards Farouk's camp.

As they entered the medical camp they were not allowed to go in freely, for these terrorist were fully aware what was going on, so they were met by Zabida a few minutes later, Farouk and the other stay indoor leaving Zabida to handle this matter.

Zabida put on a friendly and polite face as she emerged from inside, she looked pretty and innocent as a Goddess of love "good morning may I help you please" said Zabida.

"Is Doctor Vishal inside? Can I see him?" asked Britney.

"I am very sorry he is on an errand to rescue some trapped victims" said Zabida.

"To be brief I just wanted to speak to him to recall about this victim, this is her husband, so he is looking for his wife" said Britney.

"So much of hundreds of victims have been treated and left. As such no one cannot recall any face or whereabouts, I am very sorry" answered Zabida.

"Please! Please help me, she is my wife, I have looked everywhere but I can't find her, then according to this young lady here, she took out her photograph on a bed lying in this hospital that was the last of her, please I am begging" said Paul.

Zabida looked at Paul with a scorn on her face "As I said I am very sorry we can't help your situation, my advice to you check any nearby medical camp, after she may leave this camp, as you claimed she was here, she may take refuge some where for a rest, then go on her way" said Zabida.

"Oh my God, just like that she disappeared from now here" said Paul.

"I am very sorry, we helped her to regain her life\, then she must have left with some one, who trying to give her some asistance, try again, she might be some where …, somewhere, I wish you luck, by the way I am very busy" said Zabida as she disappeared into the camp leaving Britney and Paul to solve their problems.

Chapter 11

Zabida Mohammed the Angel of Death but the Goddess of beauty was so charming in looks and cunning in her soft and sweet voice made her look as innocent as a child. However her inside was like stone of cruelty and venom produced more than a cobra. This was her way of life, then she believes at times of her death she will meet with the great Allah au Ackbar her lord and live in peace and harmony like a prince or some Goddess. That is her dream and believes of heaven in some paradise for she had carried out the work her lord deserved, may the great lord have mercy upon her and her God.

At once she held a discussion among herself, Abu Farouk, Fyzal Khan and The Butcher Waheeda Hamid. They at once informed Katija the Captain of the Boat Allah Blessings to be on an alert if possible if they could escape by some means and to blow up the boat if it comes to a position leaving no trace behind at last they will reunite and some other victims will compensate for their losses.

Zabida plan inside the camp was to kidnap this child Stacy where they will receive a handsome price for her beauty, this at many times they have sold virgins to these wealthy Sheiks for hefty money. For money was no problem when they need a young virgin with good looks, thus to them Stacy Ann should fall a victim.

Then if this lover of Lucy seeking further he too will fall an easy victim. Also if possible Britney walk into the trap, she would be caught. But they reconsidered this point of Britney due to an English journalist. Then her father background as an English Captain who they wanted badly, so how they will take father and daughter, but it was a challenge, this was their main goal. They will torture that Captain until he bawl out all he knows as secret to the English navy that was Zabida's idea.

Then comes Abu Farouk, his mission was to undermine Captain Anderson Hudson and his daughter, while Zabida was the captive and organs, the both of them mission were different, but to work under one umbrella, firstly Abu Farouk came and made his way to help Zabida, who supposed to spend a few days and night load up her booty of cargoes and leave. Then Farouk will take care of his business and leave as others are pulling out of this island.

At present they had accomplished more than half their goal for Zabida almost made up her booty, then Abu Farouk had a group of young men working for him in the name of Allah, however something gone wrong by taking this Lucy as captive, ironically they are brilliant in their work, however at present they have to restructure their plan for both of their mission to be completed successfully.

All in all as they put their plan together, this child Stacy Ann would had to vanished from Haiti, this will be done easily by Farouk's idea, he claimed, he at present accomplished, where by, he had orginased a group of Haitians inhabitants about fifty men with their leader Don Diego known as Scarface, who was the gang leader.

Abu Farouk had approached him where he fell an easy victim due to the food and clothing offered to him, to be distributed to his gang and their family members, they at present were living under two large camps that Farouk had set up, he was claiming these were the casualties they rescued. Nevertheless they were his guards and thugs that he controlled. Then Scarface new name was Abdulla so were the others with Muslim names.

At present this was the gang who was his present power, at last he would leave them in Muslim faith, then gradually they will spread the Muslim faith, also later on he will finance them with a ;little capital to be come terrorists to his use later on, when need be.

At last after a long debate over their meeting to put things in place ended, their plan was reconstructed as a steel cage of a trap for their victims plans they had their defense for every movement, death to anyone that will break the silence or proven weak to answer any question weakly. Then at once Don Diego known as Scarface with the new name Abdulla was called in. there his instructions were carefully given.

Stacy Ann was left in the hands of Doctor Dale Mackintyre, Dale was busy with his casualties for bodies will fetched in stretchers non stop, however there were other doctors, but they were all busy in their job of sympathy for these victims were in pains.

As a child of six ears old, Stacy Ann was accustomed to play with children of her age, so within the camp she was much bored. Then again the nurses were busy too, so Stacy walked out of the camp to find some friends in the surrounding camp, which she displaying and having fun forgetting about her problems. This all children will do for fun of playing is their enjoyment. Here they may forget the penalties they would receive later by their parents.

At this moment Abdulla and his gang of about ten were looking for their victims to complete their job, according of their description they came upon Stacy.

Abdulla knew his instructions and the penalty for and foolish mistake, so carefully he took out a handkerchief soaked with chloroform from his pocket. Carefully with his left hand he held Stacy in a gently and polite way then placed the handkerchief on her face covering her mouth and nose, within a few seconds Stacy body became lifeless.

Abdulla lifted her up gently in his two arms in front of him to his stomach, then one of his men covered her with a blood stained cloth as if she had been just rescued as a victim, they then continued their journey with out anyone take any heed, for walking with someone bloody was nothing strange because this was what Haiti position at present was, casualties everywhere bloody seeking help.

A short distance away The Butcher was awaiting in one of Farouk's vehicle, as Abdulla placed Stacy in the vehicle he knew his job, immediately he headed for the shore-line of this island, then with a clean and fresh \ bundle in his hand his destination was to Allah Blessing.

Britney had left Paul Saxon on his duty to find his lover while she want to continue her job. Distressed Paul Saxon was heading nowhere so he decided to use money to buy information to find his lover.

At last he found a little break, for money is a means of change that could buy anything, under a large mango tree there was a group of middle aged men with some other youths. They had their means of making a living too for at present on this island "Dog eating dog" everyone have to survive in this circumstances for the weak shall perish and the strong shall survive.

Paul walked up to the group and said to them.

"A pleasant good morning friends"

A few grumbles "Good morning" while the others stayed quiet but they all looked at him for his clothing and appearance look healthy at this present time.

Paul decided top approach them again "please I need some help"

They all looked at him for everyone needed help.

"I have money to pay" said Paul.

Everyone face changed and became interested like a herd of rabbit resting then a stone fall withim, then their ears and heads up ready to listen.

"What is it" they all whispered together.

Paul looked at them then reading their face expression he took out the photograph of Lucy, an ageable strong fellow scrambled the photograph from Paul's hand. They all anxious to have a look.

Then Paul said "Does anyone of you ever see her?"

They all looked at the photograph, some closing their eyes to imagine while some gaze in space all of them just meditating in concentration.

Paul once broke the silence "she is my wife, I am looking for her, she was a mid wife at a hospital around this area, I will pay to find her"

"My friend we can't eat money, right now money have no value on this land, if you got food and water we can work for you, we will begin to tumble these rubbles of the hospital but we need food" said the strong fellow that took the photograph.

"No she is not below these rubble, she was last seen at a medical camp" said Paul as he began to describe.

"How much you could pay, I tell you something" said a young man in his early twenties, his name was Lungo but his nick name is Rat, he got this nickname from his profession of slyness.

"Depends on what I get" replied Paul.

"I am the leader of this gang, and all business should be done by me" said Kunta, the strong Fellow.

"OK Kunta, let us talk business, I will pay let us hear what this youth have to say" said Paul.

"Tell him Rat, what you know" said Kenta.

"Don Diego gang is working for that camp, all the people that are living in those camps is Don gangs members and family, what I know they already have plenty food and water and living healthy, but this is what he had to pay for, no casualties once taken to that medical camp never show up. Then during the night that Don, Scarface and his boys will burry dead bodies in that hills, but that is their business" said Lungo, known as Rat.

Paul face began to change for his lover was last seen in that camp then he said in a horse voice.

"I will leave this photograph together with my name, address and phone number, any news is money."

"How much you will pay for this?" asked Kunta.

They settled with a price and Paul pay them a little advance, leaving his call card together with the photograph and leave with an idea in his head.

His idea was to find little Stacy Ann and put her in to safely, then to discuss this with Britney to get some help.

About a little after lunch Paul find the US army camp as was described by Britney there he was met by Doctor Dale. Paul introduced himself to him including Britney. To identify Stacy Ann there was no Stacy Ann, no body could not gave account for Stacy Ann. This upset both Paul and Dale, how could she disappeared, Paul began to abuse Doctor Dale that he and Britney have some thing in common, for Lucy and Stacy Ann disappearance,.

Once again Paul Saxon become more depressed and heart broken, closer he reached to find Lucy she disappeared, then again Stacy she disappeared. However, he put determination in himself and faith in God to help these helpless individuals that he loved and shared his times together.

Before Paul Saxon leave Doctor Dale's camp he asked Dale "Doc you are an American doctor and soldier, please be honest with me, you all came here to help these people in somehow, however what is really going on this island, right now I am confused I can't see what is going on but please tell me, I begging you in the name of the almighty God"

"Mister I am an honest soldier serving as a doctor, my duty is to help and to be truthful. I personally admired that little child" replied Dale.

"So how come this child disappeared like her mother, the last she was healthy in your protection?" asked Paul.

"My friend to me, this is a mystery, the mother, Britney last saw her in a medical camp, then the next morning she disappeared, then this child was here in front of everyone, then no one saw what happen to her maybe perhaps she may walk away looking for her mother herself" replied Dale.

"Is there anyway I could get help?" asked Paul

Dale studied this question then said "I don't know what to tell you look around and see what is going on for yourself" said Dale.

"OK Doc I am going to find out something I may be back with some solution" said Paul.

"I will be waiting to help in anyway mister"

"Thank you Doc" said Paul as he walked away.

"Please remember I am here to help at any time you need me" shouted Dale.

"I will come back with some clue and some body will have to answer" said Paul over his shoulder. Worried and angry;

Chapter 12

Stacy Ann disappearance had hunt a few people who was not her blood stream, for Dale he was grieving then for Britney it was hurtful, but at last for Paul Saxon it hurt his heart for both mother and child, it was a mystery that he vow to solve, they does not at present have anyone to look for them but it was Paul duty for he loved them both.

No one except the terrorist, knew where this child was at present, The Butcher had taken her to their Ship Allah Blessing. This ship was specially built for its work. This ship was about one hundred and twenty feet long, the width about fifty feet wide, it was built especially for speed, it is made up of two large propellers with two turbine engine with enormous power for its job.

It consist of three different floors, the below was where the twin turbine engines situated, the other space of this floor was made up of small cages for human prisoners this was designed and built by these owner, the cages were made out of steel bars of four feet square, that could take two hundred prisoners for its cargo. But over crowded could take about three hundred prisoners. It was no better than a slave ship, for toilets there were mobile buckets, that each prisoner would allowed to drop its waste once a day by the supervision of their captive.

The second floor was an intensive care unit with operation rooms, also consists of large freezers to store and keep body parts alive, part of it, in a nutshell it was like a small nursing home and mortuary, here they kept body parts and organs alive, also was possible cloning of human beings, this second floor alone cost a fortune of money to furnish equipments for their theater.

The top floor that rise above the roof was life on a luxurious cruise ship, the bow was most modern design for luxury and relaxation, while the deck have a small swimming pool of ten feet by fifteen feet with a well stacked bar of expensive whisky and Champaign, this was for their joy and love making.

In the centre of the top floor was made up of luxurious cabins, a kitchen and a large table of a dining room with all luxury of furniture and computer devices name it, it worth golden money, it was insulated with both hot and cold, it was their paradise not with Allah they would enjoyed these luxuries.

However at the below floor for prisoners, there sit Mary Lucy in one of these cages, together with other captives. Then later Stacy Ann was place beside her mother in her cage, at last she found her mother.

Stacy Ann was place in her mother cage for two important reasons. They expected the prison cell to be over crowded within a few hours so they need rooms. Secondly placing Stacy Ann with her mother she will take good care of her until the time of sale.

Mary Lucy as a captive in a prison cell was grieving of her daughter safety. Then some hours later they were reunited, this gave them both a new life, juts like some animal in the slaughter house, but given her young for a last breast feeding, it was their desire for both such was Stacy Ann and her mother Mary Lucy at present in their cage, this gave them some hope and fate that a God exists. However they do not know where there future lies, yet praying to their honest God for freedom some prayers may be answered by the glorious God, while some ends up as Allah wishes.

Above all prayers to the almighty, ones God is one freedom of paradise, as prayers to an honest god is the answer to all problems, in death or life there is a promise land for liberation but all captives in a cage of this ship Allah Blessing, fate lies in the hands of the Lord Jesus Christ the holy savior.

At present the only hopes of freedom for this mother and child and the others depends on frustrated Paul Saxon determination to solve this mystery through the holy spirit of God, may God have mercy upon every soul.

Paul Saxon was a man of determination and ego, once put his mind on something he have to gain victory, he never accepted defeat in his life, he would try and try again, if not one way maybe the other, but he believed always to win and to achieve his goal such was his life style for prosperity at present.

Desperately Paul went in search for Britney for he had the money to purchase a used vehicle in this island for he was born and bred in Port=au=prince, his idea he would drive the entire island to explore his search and unravel this mystry, somewhere they may be held captive for a ransom, this he told himself he had some of uncle Sam dollars to spend for love, the one he love was his life companios.

Also on he returns from America from his last trip he came to help them, but spend all on Lucy and Stacy. So at present money was no problem for him although things were expensive and scarce, once you have money you could buy anything, so his hope was to buy Lucy and Stacy freedom.

His thoughts was, that somebody on this island had kidnapped them hoping they would receive a ransom sometimes to come.

Evening came and Paul found Britney with her camera man Bill Samson they were both busy in their daily activities.

"Good evening miss Britney" said Paul to Britney.

"Good evening Mr. Paul! Any good news?" asked Britney.

"You deceived me miss, how could you" replied Paul.

"How could you say that!" answered Britney.

"You should know why I said that" said Paul.

"Doctor Dale call me on my cell and told me that Stacy was missing" said Britney.

"So you got the news?" asked Paul.

"I am very sorry, Paul" said Britney.

"That is all you could say miss, but I am the one who is the loser and broken heart" said Paul.

"Mr. Paul I know your feelings but Doctor Dale and I both love Stacy, we were thinking about adopting her if no one showed up, she is very cute, I can't believe that bad news" said Britney.

It is very easy to sympathize, by my heart is burning for love" said Paul.

"Mister Paul please don't say that, I could do anything for Stacy such is Dale" replied Britney.

"Yet he could not take care of her" replied Paul.

"Paul, I promised there is something had to be done but how we will begin, there is no security no police to carry out their duties like that at present, this island is in mutiny badly in need of help to restore peace and health" said Britney.

"If they were dead and I see their dead bodies I would have satisfied like the others, but Lucy went missing so was Stacy she was kidnapped or some thing like that" said Paul.

"Your words hurts me but ask Bill, he could tell you the truth" said Britney calling Bill attention, "Bill"

"Yes Miss Britney" answered Bill.

"Did you see the woman on that bed where you took her photograph that I ask you for that I told you went missing" asked Britney.

"Yes she was unconscious on that bed when I took the photograph, I swear to that" said Bill.

"That I understand, but where on earth she had disappeared?" asked Paul.

"I am very sorry for this woman, but if Britney will agree we can go back to that camp and refresh their memories, may be I could take out some more photographs to show on the air and if they went missing then the world would see as such we will gain some points to be important" said Bill.

"Bill if you agree I could go back there for the third time, oh my God" said Britney.

"Agreed, can't you lend us your car, this evening before dark we shall be there" said Bill.

"You could take the car once you find something interesting" said Paul.

"OK we'll get back your car by four this evening with some good news, I promise you" said Bill.

"At your service, the keys in its place" said Paul.

"Take it cool Mr. Paul we will do some thing to help have confidence in us." said Britney.

"I have already loose confidence in everything but once I have life I will try to find my loved one, they are my life" said Paul.

"I promise you this time I will take good footage that I could give account for, my name is Bill" said Bill.

Once again Mr. Paul Saxon leave on his own with his own idea and motive, there is God by his side, have no faith in man for they will all times deceive you.

Britney at the wheel while Paul will take out some footage now and then they will stop now and then at any scene of rescue workers working to take out footage or to find out about Lucy and Stacy, yet their regular answers were no.

They were no electricity on the island for only the refugee camp built by the foreigners or red cross and other unit, the entire island was in darkness, a light on the road was a vehicle head lights, then the hills and valleys made the road sometimes difficult to drive also some places on the road was damaged or blocked with rubbles. All in all there was only a narrow road to drive on, so all drivers had to be careful.

That evening Zabida, Farouk, Fyzal khan and The Butcher Waheeda was having dinner together on a private table inside their camp at the said time their planning was going on as a formal meeting. As they were about to finish their meals, a servant report to them that the English woman and her camera man were outside, they were informed that they wanted to speak to Dr. Vishal. Together the four of them eyes met.

With a smile, the eyes contact only made and a conclusion was already there. Zabida quickly gave a sign, briskly The Butcher and Fyzal cleared the table and disappeared, and leaving Farouk and Zabida on the clean table with the two empty chairs, as the nurse went and welcome the two visitors in.

The nurse then went and gave Scarface "Abdulla" his instructions, his order was to get raid of the visitors car, the island was already in darkness, so as fast as possible Abdulla and his boys should take this car a little distance away from this medical camp, drive it down some place get it painted over with some kind of paint then some distance away it should be burnt in some valley or bushes.

This instruction was carried out immediately.

Inside the camp a conversation was going on among Zabida, Farouk, Britney and Bill.

"My England friends, please let me get your idea clearly what do you want from us, you come here for some more footage?" asked Zabida.

"Yes, and if you allowed us" said Bill.

"The last time you took some footage of photos of some victims, but clearly we can't give account for all these victims we have treated" said Farouk.

"Doc we saw a woman in your medical camp where we have some photographs, then she disappeared no one can't give am account for, then today her daughter who was in our company she also disappeared, then the woman husband is looking for her and her child, as such he told us, we are responsible for his family, and that is not true" said Britney.

"My friend it is simple the woman who was a victim was treated then left, but the child as you said was in you all care and she disappeared during the day, all as I could see you all are responsible for the child, this I can't understand only you come here to enquire about her and have more photographs of our business?" asked Zabida.

"Doc we are just trying to help solve a mystery, it just happened so fast" said Britney.

"I find you should just look around for hundreds of thousands of people are missing because of this earthquake" said Farouk.

"OK with your permission could we take some more photographs to show the world the good your medical camp is doing" said Bill.

"Maybe you must have got some footage full in your camera to show the world" said Zabida.

"OK that must be interesting, can we see some of them?" asked Zabida.

"No these are personal for our own news media" said Bill.

"OK I will show you some of our" said Zabida.

As she got up and left, briskly she disappeared behind a room, the reappeared after a few minutes then sit back in her seat, both Britney and Bill was looking at Zabida to see what she have to show them.

Waheeda and Fyzal quietly ooze for the door with a piece of clothe each in their hands, so fast they placed in on each face with the other hand on the victim head.

Within seconds the chloroform too its effect as such both Britney and Bill were out of the world.

Chapter 13

This island of Haiti that situated in the Caribbean Sea was in serious distress of the day of February 12, 2010. So were her inhabitants. Also one who visited this island felt the same broken hearted, except a few who will gain a profit of the loss of the people. However, if there was no sick patient there would be no work for a Doctor, similarly if there is no crime, there is no use of policemen and lawyers, yet again these people of Haiti need help for all of us are human beings, no advantages should be taken upon these helplessness, adding more pains on their miseries, then aded to other tears for their pains while some on their bending knees praying to God to have mercy upon them, truly they are in pains and humanitarians should shared their grief because all of us may need a helping hand at some intervals to come.

Similarly as Paul Saxon was broken hearted for these last few days, such was Doctor Dale Macintyre, for he had some how have a feeling and likeness for this child, then the guilt tightened his heart for due to his negligence somebody had taken this innocent and quiet child from his grip, yet he decided to do something for her, but this was not his duty, then again where he will start if he was going to help; there was no law on this island at present, there were only rescue teams volunteering to help to save lives in all ways.

There were soldiers to maintain the law of peace. So at this time it was impossible to solve the mystery of a missing mother and a child. This will be much ridiculous for thousands are missing in different ways.

Doctor Dale Mackintyre could feel his stomach tightened with sympathy for these inhabitants especially Stacy Ann. He decided to put the challenge to major Ashton Benn to help his daughter in some way, some how he felt this child need help, then he knew who the father was, so why not let him know what happening to his daughter.

To get major Briggs interested in helping he made sure he found Stacy bloody clothing, that she had came into his army medical camp, so that major Briggs as a doctor could run a DNA test, in this way if the test prove positive for surety he will be willing to help, if not the test prove negative he will find another way to gain help for this child. That evening with Stacy Ann's blood stained clothing in a parcel in his hand he went to pay major Briggs another visit.

Entering Major Briggs's cabin he was greeted with a welcome by Major Briggs "You are an impressive doctor, soldier boy, you get everything in place"

"Sorry to say major, Bad News!" said Dale.

Major Briggs rocked back in his chair and gave Dale a queer look, peering Dale brains to read for answers.

"What do you mean by bad news?" asked Major Ashton.

"Dale was looking back directly into major Ashton eyes to read his reality to his last few words, thinking how to catch him down to accept this child so he may help in some way.

Two smart doctors were trying to exploit one another intellect for an answer, then major Ashton Briggs asked "What is your encounterment, for surgery, bad news my friend"

"Stacy Ann has disappeared" said Dale slowly.

"Disappeared! How?" asked major Ashton as he rocked back in his chair.

"That is interesting major" replied Dale.

"Doctor Dale I really can't understand what is taking place at this time with you in my personal affairs" said Major Ashton Briggs.

"It is all a sad story to relate major" said Dale.

"If you speak I am willing to listen" answered Major Briggs.

"It is most disappointed agenda, I even involved in, but trust me, my words are true, and we need your help! Me and Stacy before it is too late" said Dale.

"Please tell me your disappointed idea?" asked Major Ashton.

"The child just disappeared, just as her mother had. I don't know this means to your major" said Dale.

"If I knew for certain the child is mine then I will do my duty as a father should Doctor" said Major Ashton.

"Before it is too late major, in my hands is the equation to solve the doubt" said Dale with a pale voice.

"What is you equation Doctor?" asked Major Ashton.

Placing the parcel on major Ashton table in front of him Dale said "this is the child's blood stained clothing, with this you could definitely know the answer to all your questions major" said Dale.

"Doctor Ashton Briggs took the parcel and said "I promised you this, if I am the father then count on me, immediately I am going to get the DNA done and if the child is mine you will not need my help, I will definitely need your help, you promised me that doctor" said major Ashton Briggs as he was already standing on his feet.

"Thank you major, I am counting on you"said Doctor Dale as he was leaving"

"Our words ware our promise" replied Major Ashton Briggs.

"Be a dedicated father to your child major" said Dale as he was closing Major Ashton cabin door.

Britney Hudson and her cameraman Bill Samson became captives, as been drugged by these terrorists they were stripped nude for any devices hidden in their clothing, thus their clothing were burnt for no trace if any, as for the camera the professions scanned thoroughly to ensure there was no device also, but the footage was inside was kept, if at any time the need any photographs for their purpose.

The both of them were transported to the ship Allah Blessing the said night as nude as they were born, but as they were on their transport journey they were covered with blood stained clothing, this reasons if seem by anyone, these terrorist would claim that they were earthquake victims and at present they were casualties in their hands for medical treatments.

Britney was awaken from her consciousness in a steel cage unknown to her, she was in a sitting position nude, her body was supported by her back to the small iron bars, by her feet was a small blanket if she needed to cover her nude body.

Awaken to her real life she was stunned to find herself in this position, at first she told herself that she was dreaming lost in some nightmare, back within minutes she became reflective then realized this was no dream. She quickly took the nasty blanket and cover herself, wrapped like a kitten in comfort of warmth. She then positioned her self to relax and think what was happening.

In the dim light of the ship compartment on her left to her in a next cage was a woman and a child, on her right was another healthy negro girl, what she could see opposite her were cages with other human beings in crouching positions some sleeping.

She thought of Bill, but could not see him in any cage that her eyes could focus on, and then her attention was drawn to the woman and child next to her, so she slowly whispered to the woman,

"Hello" the body of the woman move not to disturb the child comfort for the cage was too small for the two of them comfort, yet she tried to make it comfortable for there was nothing she could do as a prisoner.

As the woman moved her head Britney once again whispered "Hello"

The woman open her eyes staring at her. Britney as an educated journalist have to act in a smart way to know what was happening and to have some idea where she was at present.

"What is your name" whispered Britney.

The woman was confused and shocked seeing this happenings for the last two and three days. Do not know who speak to for to her no one was a friend.

"What is your name? Please" whispered Britney the woman get staring at her in the dim light in astonishment.

"Please let us be friends, may be we could help each other" whispered Britney.

"Who are you?" whispered the woman.

"My name is Britney Hudson; I am an English journalist working from the BBC news media in England. Friend please talk to me so I could know where am I, may be I could help you too" said Britney.

The woman looked at Britney with a disappointed face then slowly whispered with a hoarse voice of pains.

"No body can help us as far I could see; only God can"

"Please don't give up, there could be help, my father is an English major of the army, once he find that I am missing he will look for me" said Britney.

"OK miss my name is Mary Lucy and this here sleeping with me is my daughter Stacy Ann" whispered the woman.

Britney covered her mouth with the back of her hand with wide open eyes then whispered

"Oh my God! Poor Stacy Ann, she is my friend"

"So you know my poor child?" asked Lucy.

"Yes she is my friend, she was stolen from us as we were looking for you" said Britney.

"That is your friend too, he is a white man they brought the two of you naked a few hours ago" said Stacy pointing to the cell next to her.

Britney raised her hand to look in the cell next to Lucy, there she could see Bill in a crouching positing yet asleep without clothes.

Britney memories began to flow back from where she could remember.

"Oh my great God, he is in here too, I could remember the two of us were looking for you, that was the last, then I woke up in this prison" said Britney.

"So you know who brought you here?" asked Lucy.

"Yes I have and idea" replied Britney.

"So you believed we could get help?" asked Lucy.

Britney at a sudden looked at Stacy with a bright face with open eyes wide, then said "You know someone by the name of Paul Saxon?"

Life came to Mary Lucy face, at once she whispered."Yes, he is my boyfriend, and do you know him?"

"Yes, he is looking for you, we supposed to meet with him this evening, but we ended up here" said Britney.

"So he will find you missing too?" asked Lucy.

"Yes he will look for us, then perhaps when find out we are missing he would contact Doctor Dale, at once Dale will inform my father" then Britney voice slow down in a dead surprise.

"What is it? Is something gone wrong?" asked Lucy.

"Suppose they hold him captive too, then our hopes are shattered" said Britney.

"No! my friend, you don't know Paul he is stubborn he never gives up hopes and if he knew we are alive and missing he will find us, he love me as he love his own life, he will do anything for me and my child" said Lucy as she broke down in tears.

Britney felt her heart for Lucy, she felt like hugging her in her arms, but the iron bars separated them, what she did to show her sympathy she placed her hand through the bar in friendship Lucy held hers as she was yet weeping.

With the vibration of Lucy's body Stacy Ann woke up with a groan of "Mama, mama"

As Stacy wake up from her sleep, Britney whispered "Stacy Ann! Stacy is me, miss Britney"

Hearing Britney's voice Stacy stared to look at Britney who was looking as a witch in a corner.

"That is Miss Britney, your friend Stacy?" said Lucy.

"Mamma Miss Britney is my friend" said Stacy.

"Where is Doctor Dale, Miss Britney?" asked Stacy.

"He is at the medical camp" said Britney.

"Will he look for us? Miss Britney" asked Stacy.

"Definitely! He will Stacy" answered Britney.

"Will he find us?" asked Stacy.

"Pray to God and he will send Doctor Dale and Mr. Paul to us" said Britney.

"Uncle Paul is looking for Mama Miss Britney" Asked Stacy.

"Yes honey, don't be scared uncle Paul and Doctor Dale will find us" answered Britney.

Stacy Ann too developed more courage and hopes holding her mother chin with her hands she said, "Mama don't cry, place mama, some one will help us"

"My child only God have to help us" said Lucy yet sobbing.

"Mama stop crying and let us pray to God" said Stacy.

Lucy was looking down as Stacy with the tears in her eyes.

Then Stacy began the prayers "Our father who arth in heaven" she was then joined by Britney, then next verse Lucy joined in they were all whispering their prayers.

Then the sound of a metal door as heavy keys were rattling on it.

Chapter 14

Mr. Paul Saxon had expected to hear some news from Britney and her cameraman Bill Samson, also his car was borrowed. After the time that was given to him went past, he just went about his way for Britney ideas was some kind of sham. At this point he cared less about these foreigners for they are un-confidential and they took his car for their own purpose. But some how in the morning they will have to return his car for his lover and her daughter have to be found.

The next morning came and Paul Saxon was looking for his car, not for any news from Britney, because Paul by now was losing his temper in many unanswered questions, and yet he was still at the beginning, no a clue to any answer, however this mother and child have to be found.

Hours past and yet no answer so Paul decided to hear what the American army Doctor Dale Mackintyre have to say over this situation.

At last Paul met with Doctor Dale.

"Good morning Mr. Paul" said Dale with a sad face.

"Good morning doc, how are you?" answered Paul.

"Not to bad my friend, what about you?" asked Dale.

"Doc, what is really going on, please tell me something, I lost my lover, then the child in your protection, then yesterday I lent Britney my car and it look like I have lost my car too" said Paul with a sad face.

With Paul's statement Dale face becomes paler, in amazement he asked, "What you just said, Britney and your care are missing?"

"Yes, she borrowed my car yesterday to visit the Medical camp where Mary Lucy was last seen. Britney promised me she will return my car by nine o'clock last night, up to now I can't find her" replied Paul.

"Then she went missing too?" whispered Dale.

"Well yes. So far I can't find her, also my car went missing too, what the hell is going in my life" said frustrated Paul Saxon.

Doctor Dale was looking in the sky for and answer scratching his chin with his fingers talking to himself "yesterday Stacy Ann disappeared, and then in the evening Britney Hudson disappeared, this is not good, something gone wrong"

"Doc, please tell me something, you are studying your sweet heart disappearance what about my car" said Paul.

"I will pay you for your car, but you will have to help me find Britney" said Dale.

"Doc please listen to me, I all have something to do with that medical camp where Lucy was last seen" said Paul.

"Paul be patient with me, why you said that about the medical camp?" asked Dale.

Paul explained his meeting with the group of Kunta and Lungo, then with Lucy disappearance then yesterday Britney and her cameraman was to visit that camp in the evening, God knows what happen" said Paul.

With interest Dale said to Paul "so that medical camp are linked with the terrorists"

"As far as I am concerned they had inhabited and dominated a gang working for them under the leadership of "Scarface" Don Diego"

According to Kunta and Lunga they say these gangs taking body to the medical camp, then taking other bodies out of the camp and buried them, then they provided shelter only for the gang members only, no one else think about it Doc" said Paul.

Dale became interesting at once" so there is already a terrorist group that invade this island at this sad times!" he said.

"It had to be because people are been disappeared suddenly?" said Paul.

"OK Paul if Britney is missing we will contact her father major Anderson Hudson of the English navy, he will investigate this matter because of her daughter and an English or American citizens must be answered for on this island" said Dale.

"So what we do standing here and talking or we should find out the truth" said Paul.

"Excuse me for a minute, let me have a talk with my superior, then we will have a vehicle for our business" said Dale as he disappeared inside the camp.

Dale return in a haste with his army uniform fully equipped with his gun at his hip, then a motion for Paul to follow he mounted a small army jeep, as the both headed to the English Navy camp to Major Anderson Hudson office.

Arriving at the British navy camp, Doctor Dale was welcome as a soldier on duty Dale waste no time at once he and his companion was seated in major Anderson office explaining their errand.

"When was the last time you saw your daughter Britney, major?" asked Dale.

"The evening before yesterday Doc, she was here with a child" answered Major Anderson.

"Do you saw her anytime yesterday evening on this morning?" asked Dale.

"Why something strange had happen to her?" asked Major Anderson.

"The child you saw with her had been kidnapped or disappeared yesterday anytime about lunch time yesterday, that child is Mr. Paul who sitting here step child. Her mother was last seen in St. Mark in a medical camp, Britney had a footage of her resting in the camp then she disappeared, then yesterday Britney and her camera man borrowed Mr. Paul car to visit that medical camp, they were supposed to meet back with Mr. Paul for nine o'clock last night, but unfortunately Britney and her cameraman and the car also disappeared" said Dale.

"What! Britney disappeared, impossible! said Major Anderson.

"Yes sir, believe me please" said Paul.

Do you checked by her office?" asked Anderson.

"Yes sir I looked everywhere for her to get my car to do my business, but I can't find her" said Paul.

"That is impossible" said Major Anderson.

"Can't believe it sir, but I can lead you to other evidence, to prove that camp is suspicious of kidnapping human beings" said Paul

"Yes I believe you about terrorist invading certain countries for body organs and trafficking of human beings in different business, this we encountered in Afghanistan and other countries, but I can't believe they have already set up camp in this island, already operating" said Major Anderson.

"Yes sir, believe me, they took my lover and her daughter this I will lead you to a gang, if you have money to pay for information" said Paul.

"If my daughter is missing I have to find her, it is my duty top protect my citizens" said Major Anderson.

"Major we will have to do something before it is too late" said Doctor Dale.

"OK where are they taking those hostages, this island is so small?" asked Major Anderson.

This we have to investigate major" said Dale.

"If I lead you to this gang led by Kunta, he will lead you to everything, so you will have an idea where to start your investigation" said Paul.

"OK we have no choice we have to do something briskly to be ahead" said Major Anderson.

They found themselves in St. Mark about lunch time, the sun was heated, but the daily activities was going on with the rescue workers busy to save lives, but at present for these few days gone by life become as usual with the screams of human beings in pains as rescue team dug out trapped and living people below rubbles,

On the other hand the one survived the earthquake problem was to find food and water so there was a busy daily activities for most while the men who formed their themselves into gangs will gather in their groups planning some ways to obtain food and clothing or water for their surviving family.

Doctor Dale driving with Paul and major Anderson Hudson was indeed in St. Mark looking for a break way to solve a mystery. Paul saw his new friends of Haitian Kunta and his boys below the said mango tree by the road side, it seems that this was their office of gathering and planning.

Paul told Doctor Dale to stop so he Paul could have a few words as was promised, so Paul walked to Kunta and his boys as Dale and Anderson sit in the army vehicle waiting.

"Good day friends; you have any information for me?" asked Paul.

"We have plenty news, but we don't know if you have the money to pay for all" said Kunta.

"Good or bad news?" asked Paul.

"Those are your friends?" asked Kunta as he pointed to Dale and Anderson.

"Yes! They wanted to know about something I am paying for" said Paul.

"Well they are American and English Soldiers they controlled food, water and clothing, they can help pay! Call them" said Kunta.

"Before I call them let me know one good news? said Paul.

"We saw a burnt up car concerning the white girl with your girl friend photograph. You want to know more, you can, but first pay because we worked whole night last night to know all this, so we were looking for you, so tell your friends to come and listen. Maybe the white girl concerning them then if they pay good we will help find her" said Kunta.

"So you know where she is?" asked Paul.

"We can tell you, maybe you can find your girlfriend too" said Kunta.

Paul leave Kunta and his boys and walked up to Dale and Anderson. Then said to them "these people have some news, they said they know where to find Britney" said Paul.

"Who are they" asked Major Anderson.

"I hired them yesterday" said Paul.

"You hired them? For what?" asked Major Anderson.

"To find Stacy Ann and Lucy!" said Paul

"Do you believe in them?" asked Major Anderson.

"I have to, that is why I pay them because I want to find my family safely" said Paul.

"Major please let us listen to what they have to say" said Doctor Dale.

"But they want payment for their news" said Paul.

"What types of money?" asked Dale.

"Food and water included clothing, if not you can pay them money so they will go and buy food?" said Paul

"OK let us hear what they have to offer for we have water and food in abundance to give away so this is free news for us" said Major Anderson.

Major Anderson lead they way forwards, below the mango tree to meet the native gang of "gang men" good day gentlemen" greeted the group, by Major Anderson.

The group responded by "good day sir"

"OK gentlemen, I have offered food, water, clothing and even whisky as payment, but my facts must be truth, no lies" said Major Anderson.

"Whisky, whisky" whispered each individual then Kunta said directly to major Anderson, we saw what we are telling you, sir after this mister pay we well yesterday we kept a whole night and day watch on Scarface and his gang also on the medical camp. We went so far, that we know that they hired Scarface and his gang, and changed Scarface name to Abdulla" said Kunta.

"Abdulla" whispered Major Anderson then said this is Muslims operations.

"Yes sir most of the gang names have been to Muslims, then any thing they do they did "in the name of Allah" said Kunta.

"Tell me do you see any white girl with a white guy show up around here yesterday" asked Dale.

"Yes sir, we have a watch group over there at present, Ants and three others are spying on them, when Ants and his group return a next four will keep a next eye on them. This is what this Mr. Paul paid us for, but we did saw the white girl and her companion a white big belly fella went in the camp yesterday, as the night got dark we never saw them come out, but their car is down that valley burnt" said Kunta.

"Who burnt the car?" asked Paul.

"As soon as these whites enter the medical campo Scarface and a few of his boys paint the car into a different colour then push it up that hill, then they drove it to that valley where they burnt it, this we followed on foot to see all this" said Kunta.

"So what happens to the white girl and her companion?" asked Major Anderson.

"We saw a vehicle drove out the compound some time later we believe the girl and her companion were in it, because the vehicle returns this morning in the dark and yet we see nothing about them" said Kunta.

"You have any idea where they been taken?" asked Major Anderson in a cool voice.

"No! But Scarface and his gang usually buried body at the foot of that hill, but we look this morning, but no white body" said Kunta.

Dale looked at Major Anderson; both looked at one another face for answers. Then Doctor Dale whispered "terrorists" in a low and slow voice.

Major Anderson gives a side glance and shook his head as a "yes"

"Do you know if they have a next medical camp anywhere else" Asked Major Anderson.

"We heard they have a big ship in the sea, where they are taking these people" said Kunta.

"Could you take us to the car so that Paul could indentify the car to see if it is his?" asked Dale.

"Yes, with pleasure, this is what we are working for to show the truth, so that we can get pay" said Kunta.

Kunta joined the army vehicle as they headed for its destination.

Upon examination the car, Paul was satisfactory sure that this was the exact car, the model and many other things he could identify no matter it was burnt up.

So as a result Kunta and his boys telling the truth and they had worked for their money for a break in this mystery.

Before Anderson leave he made arrangements with Kunta and his boys that as army jeep will drop their payments, also they will continue to work for them.

Any news they know where to find them and their payments.

Chapter 15

The English journalist Britney was praying with Lucy and Stacy when the keys were rattling on its position, their visitor was the ship Captain Professor Katija Ali.

At the time Britney was brought in a few hours ago she and a few of her team were busy in an operation cloning some human beings on the second floor. These professors were always busy in their occupation for their experiments to develop their profession no matter how much lives they take to develop a theory they don't care for a human life means nothing to them, once they cleared a doubt of ideas to the future a step further in their doctorate, as a result they must be the best in science.

They also cloned human beings in to human robots for suicide bombers in attacks formidable, never the less this is their taste in life for God had created them all to roam the face of this earth, but on the other hand if they had God in them and do their education ability to help people that needed help it would have been a wonder.

This Captain Katija Ali, had heard about Britney the bait to catch that major, so as she finished her business she decided to have a good look at her to decided Britney's fate in the future, once she was in their hands. Also Farouk and Zabida were having a good time on the fist floor in the bathing pool with some expensive whisky washing away their sins and their love making. Thus they wanted to have a look at Britney who was in her steel cage before they left in the morning, as the sunrise to their medical camp on the island.

As the steel door bust open everyone in their full sense awaken, they all began tremble in fright so was Britney, but seeing this pretty Goddess of beauty, Britney felt relief for she told herself this was some maid fell victim and maybe she could be polite, as she look like a morning rose from the fresh dew.

Katija walked up to Britney's cell and stop, looking at Britney wrapped like a frightened kitten in a corner "You must have been Britney" she said in a cool voice"

Britney sitting in her captive cage, give her a pleasant smile to develop friendship.

Katija's face suddenly changed to the devil, the prettiness was yet there, but became harsh, she kick the cage so it gave a hard sound staring at Britney she said "answer me when I speak to you, get up on your feet you bitch"

Britney was looking at Katija trying to read her facial expression.

"Like you want to see my power" said Katija as she placed the key in the lock to open the cell gate.

Katija then opened the gate wide, took her right hand placed her fingers on Britney's throat with a brist jurk, she had Britney on her feet as the blanket fell to the floor exposing the nude body once more. Britney tried to shake Katija hands off her neck, so swiftly Katija with her fighting combat training flung Britney to the walls a few times, Britney spine shivered in pain.

Stacy saw this and began to cry but Lucy criddle her to her bosom hiding her face in comfort.

Katija them pulled Britney out of her cell nude pushing her in the walkway, Katija said "Walk! If you decided to give me a hard time, you will be sorry for I have many use for you, you hear me Bitch!"

Katija right hand behind Britney's neck to the back as she was pushing her where she wanted her. Katija led her to the second floor as Britney looked what was going on there, her stomach became upset and her knees got weak. That was the worst stage she even saw human beings body parts in display. hearts, kidneys, lungs etc, all types and kinds of body parts under some device alive.

Katija then took her up the top luxurious floor with a different smell and atmosphere.

At once she remembered the luxurious hotels and cruise ship she had dwell among, but today she was a captive who could not hide her own nakedness. She was taken straight to the swimming pool where Farouk and Zabida were nude bathing having love fun, at this time Farouk and Zabida were having an enjoyable sex when she appeared.

When they finished Katija said "You want to see this bitch, here she came?" she then gave Britney a sudden push into the pool.

Zabida, move towards Britney who was standing in the pool.

"You want to share with us" she said.

Britney was trying to wash her dirty skin as Zabida held her in a kiss, Britney pulled away, Zabida then pushed her head bellow the water, then within a few long seconds she raised her head above the water.

Britney began to cough while Farouk and Zabida looking on laughing having their own fun while Britney was in her own pain of humiliation.

"You want some fun with her, Abu Farouk" asked Zabida.

"Who wants fun with an English Bitch, she will do good in some wealthy Sheik bed" said Farouk.

"I do believe she will keep him warm and comfortable for his money" said Zabida.

Britney was looking at handsome Dr Vishal for she realized this doctor who appearance was like the idol of a Roman God, that she almost fell in love heels over head with, at first he was so courteous and charming, but at present he was a handsome and cunning animal and his name was not Vishal, but Abu Farouk a terrorist.

"Take your first chance with her if you want some fun with her, perhaps you may enjoy an English slut" said Zabida.

"I don't want no English journalist in my bed, all I want is a professor like myself not a slut like her" said Farouk.

"Wash yourself clean bitch, no one wants you because you are to low in life to your stage to have fun with but at least you worth some money so please stay pretty before I change you into something else that you won't like" said Zabida.

"You find we should clone her?" asked Farouk

"When times come, we will see the best what we will make her, for now keep her alive" said Zabida.

"When I got that major under my invisible chains I will make good love with you while he look on to see what he had made" said Farouk

"Get her out of this pool" said Zabida.

"Bitch, get yourself some good clothes over there in that locker to stay pretty for the right time" said Farouk.

Britney was taking all these insults from her captors because she was a captive and the safety of her life was in their hands, for she realized that they were not human with love, but someone life means nothing to them, it was like slaughter a goat or a sheep for a good meal or fete.

She obeyed by taking her time in getting out of the pool and found some comfortable clothes in their locker; she does not bother to look for any underwear but simply pull or a pair of jeans and an ordinary jersey just to be comfortable.

Abu Farouk found himself in an expensive robe to cover his nakedness and to be comfortable.

"Hay young lady I will take you back to your prison, there you should make yourself comfortable, I do believe that will be your home for a good while" said Farouk.

Britney remained silent for she realized her new life was to take order as a captive. As she took a\good look at the open sea there were the lights of the other ships that anchored in the waters of Hati. In her thoughts she can't reconignised any friendly ship, so that she could send a message by the angel of the night.

To her idea, the time was about two o'clock in the morning. She then looked towards to the devastated island that was in darkness and her only hope of help lies and said to herself, would I ever will set foot on that island again as a free individual?

Within a few seconds she heard Abu Farouk voice.

"Walk in front bitch I will follow, I am sure you know the way to your new home, because you have walked that path to up here"

Slowly and carefully she began to walk as Farouk followed behind her heels, descending the steps to the second floor Farouk said

"Stop for a minute and look around, you claim to be a media reporter so look around and you will report to your God" said Abu Farouk.

Britney stopped to look at the horrible scene then Farouk said "Some of these bodies are dead, this is how we spread bacterial disease, we created a diseases in them, then take their dead tissue to make a fluid that we inject in people like you, then place twelve like you in England alive then there will be an outbreak of a new deadly disease that could destroy the entire England in one month because they do no have the cure for it, but the good thing about it, we have the cure for what we have created it, do you realize how much money we could make by selling our drugs for the cure, or if not just sit and watch millions of you suffer in pains awaiting death as the disease spread.

Britney looked at Farouk with no hopes in life again, but wish if this entire ship could blow to pieces to see millions of innocent lives could be in jepordy by these terrorists, tears flowed to her eyes, but with determination she held it back not to show fear.

Farouk then pointed to a few human with tubes in their body he said ''These have already injected with the virus; it will be a catching disease by breathing the air they exhale''.

"Britney close her eyes saying to herself "Oh God some scientists are bursting their brains to cure people to make this world a better place to live and look at these people they are creating pains in people lives",

Britney open her eyes and speak after a longtime of silence "Why are you doing all of this? what do you want?"

"The people in this world are our enemy, so we will slowly destroy them" said Abu.

"What have they done to be you enemies?" asked Britney.

"Please don't question me because you are not qualified to ask any question, but I am only granting you the privilege to witness our power over our enemies.

"Can I step forward to my prison?" asked Britney because she was in a state of shock, wanted to just sit down somewhere by herself to do some thinking, her stomach and head were in some state of aches and pains.

"No I just wasn't you to see one more thing" pointing to the end of the ship where some beds were occupied with partitions with tube feeding holes of their bodies "These are so ready for the Americans who believe that they are a super power, but we want to show them they are not, no body and the money they have, they should utilize it to save their own people rather than interfere in someone else's business, their government does not value their soldiers' lives to send by thousands to Afghanistan to face death and leaving remains to their families so we will torture them easily with pains"

Britney looked at him for his words, she wanted to know what are those human beings purpose.

Farouk could foresee the questions in her eyes, he let out a low whistle, then a chuckle of laughter with joy he said "Those people down there are specially cloned, they will be something like vampires carrying a deadly virus"

Britney's eyes and mouth were wide open to hear the answer but did not say a word just looking at Farouk eyes and smiling face to know what their ideas were.

Slowly Farouk continued his speech "these people have contaminated a special virus worse than AIDS, fifty two of them will be placed in each states of America, when we finish with them they will look like pretty white females in their early twenties, they will be like the human robots where a deadly virus will be transmitted through their saliva and sweat, these young females first job is to bite their first victim with a special eye-teeth to inject the virus to its vicinity by her saliva.

The victim will contaminate the virus then spread it by sex. Their sweat contact and mostly their saliva so easily, their other victims will spread the virus so within a month millions of people will be spreading the virus epidemic, above all we have the cure if this virus spread out of hands, then we will control it to suit its environment.

Britney's brains began to spin in her head. Farouk was looking at her with joy as she was in a world of pain.

Farouk continued "Then the American scientists will be fighting to build a formula to control this virus yet there will be billions of dollars to be made to sell our cure to them, but this will not happen, that will be the end of their world, as they get weaker we will invade as we are today, Foolish Americans betraying the foolish British"

"Please place me in my cell for I am at present a prisoner" said Britney.

"Which one of those patients you will like to be? You have a choice, and that is the only choice you have in your life at present for your freedom is to spear a virus"

Britney looked at Farouk and began to walk towards the steps to the bottom floor "that is a very good idea you suppose to be in your new home by now, because it is getting late at four o'clock we supposed to be back at the camp to trap that major, your father!" said Farouk.

Britney walked toward to her prison as Farouk followed he then open the cage closed it and hurried away for his job.

Chapter 16

The destructive earthquake had finished its job as a mission then gone its way, leaving everything as a chaos, on that devastated island; in the eyes of man tear drops also watered this soil while the various screams and cries followed the shadow of this destructive elements.

Ultimately, kind hearted people came to help in solidarity to share these pains of victims and help in what so ever way they could in rendering assistance to those needed, yet behind those dark clouds and dusts, hidden some monsters to terrorize and torture those people who were already in pains.

On this island Major Ander Hudson, face was stoned red with the weather, but his heart was burning with pains for his only child who had suddenly disappeared, for this major knew when a journalist or a soldier disappeared and be held captive what is their outcome of pains will be, it will be some form of torture, this he could see his daughter in his vision shouting in pains as such this will eat him internally to death, thus he would become more cruel as he was at present.

Major Anderson Hudson in command of the British camp in Haiti went back to his camp office, there he began his plan for his rescue of Britney and others who may be held captive in the hands of the unknown enemies. The first he summoned to his office was a fresh major who had got his rank a few months ago so she was under Major Anderson who was expected to be given a higher rank in a short while to sergeant major.

Major Lesa Clintwood, she was in her early thirties of thirty-two years, she was a white born in London but after graduated from college she joined the army which was her dreams to become a soldier, at an early age she had the habit of a "tom boy" so because of that her ambition was to become a soldier, she always kept her hair cut as short as possible for many reasons, from drying after taking a bath, then do away with the chores of combing a hair style, however she had the feature of a male.

At the last year in college she joined a gym then self defense class, this she enjoyed, the most of gaining a black belt in karate and judo of self defense; in this career she had fought many tournaments, as such she won more than her class, with this proudness she did not hesitate to join the army. At this time she was proud of her figure of no waste fat but muscles.

Lesa figure looks was five feet eleven inches at a medium built of weight of one hundred and fifty pounds of muscles and bone when she joined the army, this she promised to up keep under a military training.

Fortunately for Lesa she found herself comfortable in the regiment and worked her way to Captain Lesa Clintwood when she was sent in Afghanistan in command of a small platoon.

Bad luck started for Captain Lesa Clintwood and her platoon, one night in Afghanistan, her platoon had consisted of fifteen soldiers, a corporal and a sergeant while she was in command as Captain. They had their camp pitched with sentries planted, that evening a storm arose with the wind and sand everywhere this they were not much accustomed of, but they had gotten acquainted with this storm, but yet it was some of their enemies.

The storm started about eight o'clock that dark night, but lasted for a few hours, this they fought to stay alive and safe, then the fatal blow of death came, it was the attack of the Taliban. These Taliban knew how to attack for they could read the weather and lived in it for they were born in this desert storm of sands.

As the storm was about to clear up, then came these enemies with their head tied up and their faces covered, as they appeared the remembrance of all those soldiers vision came to early western movies of apache attack.

These Taliban enemies began their attack from the wind side; they were a band of over sixty fighters. As the opposite guns lit up the atmosphere under the flying sounds was like fire works appearing below the earth.

Under Captain Lesa Clintwood command they fought well, but they were out numbered by the enemies, the enemies with the help of the flying sand invaded the English army camp, there Lesa and few of her men became captives. They were taken to the Taliban camp up some hill, her men were tortured the bawl all their life in screams to death, Lesa was raped by all the Taliban, they were so much that she could not remember a count of them, she was then kept naked in a cave nude, feed like and animal, then continued to be raped as the Talibans desired.

Ironically Captain Lesa kept her self alive with the screams of her soldiers in her ears. She wanted to leave this prison alive, with her prayers and determination, she stayed alive for about two weeks, then a combined army of English and American troops under the command of Major Anderson Hudson made an attack on this Taliban camp. It was a horrible and determined battle. The Taliban's were running out of arms so they were forced to flee the mountain, leaving their prisoner Captain Lesa Clintwood behind.

Her safety and freedom was liberated by Major Anderson and his men, so to herself she owed some thing to Major Anderson.

She was then given a promotion as major and remained in major Anderson troops as a diver on board that English Army Ship. Then at last she found herself in Haiti not in a battlefield, but to render some assistance and protection. Above all she was advancing her skill of self defense which becomes her hobby. This she told herself she will get rid of those horrible visions in Afghanistan.

When summoned to Major Anderson office major Lesa was brisk and prompt to take orders from her superior major Anderson Hudson.

As Lesa took her seat opposite her superior he explained his problems, as such he was seeking her advice as being a female captive.

"Do you have any idea where she is being held captive?" asked Lesa.

"According to information she and others are prisoners on board a ship in the sea at present." answered Major Anderson.

"They are so many ships anchored in that sea at present." said Lesa.

"It is a special ship we will have to identify but for sure we know the owners of the ship." replied Anderson.

"So let us begin to trace them" said Lesa.

"We have the Haitians tacking them on land, but in that water we will have to be sure whish is our target and very fast" said Anderson.

"What is your idea major?" asked Lesa.

"We will seek the help of our friends the Americans" said Anderson.

"But we have our ship afloat on that water onboard are divers who could secretly intrude on the suspected ship." said Lesa.

Major Anderson looked into Lesa face then studied her carefully then said "Will you take care on that onboard of our ship while I personally will get the facts on land."

"That is a good idea and please depend on me, this I will do with joy to free your daughter" said Lesa.

"I hope it is not a debt you are trying to pay back to me, because we are all soldiers vowed to serve our country and pledge to look one another back" said Anderson.

"No! No! This is my duty as command, by the way you did not tell me who have your daughter in captivity?" asked Lesa.

"According to sources it is the Taliban from Afghanistan" said Anderson with a sad voice.

Lesa rose from her seat with some vigor, looking deep into major Anderson blue eyes and said, "Major! This is a joy, fun for me; this is my challenge to die for my revenge. I swear to you major what is coming for them is not good. Please promise me permission to kill to save your daughter and the other captives for I know what they will go through" said Lesa as her eyes watered and face changed to death.

"Permission is granted! But please take it cool" said Anderson.

"Major have full confidence in me" said Lesa as she got up and walked away, for she knew her task ahead.

Doctor Dale Mackintyre went to see Doctor Ashton Benn. Doctor Ashton was busy in the intensive care unit as all the specialist in doctorate to help save some lives in their profession.

Dale with a tired face had approached doctor Benn. Benn looked at Dale and thought to himself, what this young doctor wanted from him, it is all his personal life and Dale is trying to interfere in his privacy, then said "Doctor, what news you have brought me?"

"Doctor Ashton it is very important. Can I see you in private please?" asked Dale.

"What is this one, soldier boy?" asked Doctor Ashton.

"Please it is very important, lives are involved, innocent people perished and this we can do something to save them" said Dale.

OK as a military team member I will try to assist as to what you ask Doctor Dale"

They both walked to Ashton office and cabin, they both took their seat. Then Doctor Ashton said "let me hear your stories that is so important"

"I don't know if you know this young British female journalist Britney Hudson, the daughter of Major Anderson Hudson of the British army, I do believe we all fought together in Afghanistan together" said Dale.

Doctor Ashton looked at Dale then said "Yes, I know both of them; we have met in Afghanistan as you said, and by the way what is the problem with them?"

"They have got Britney" said Dale.

"Who they?" asked Doctor Ashton.

"The said ones that took your Haitian child's mother and her child" said Dale.

"What is the hell is going on Doctor, are you an FBI or an army doctor, please tell me straight up what is all this?" asked Doctor Ashton.

"Please listen to me and understand what is going on, there are some Muslim medical camp out there, they took your girlfriend, then your daughter, Britney knew about all this, then she tried to help, but some how they kidnapped her and took her to their ship" said Dale.

"So why don't you and Major Anderson try to call in some law to stop these people" said Doctor Ashton.

"They are Muslims, they came all those miles across the Atlantic ocean to this island to spread their disease and take advantages over poor individuals" said Dale.

"So what do you want me to do?" asked Benn.

"I need your help, to help those people who you and me love and don't lie to me from the bottom of your heart" said Dale.

"OK I am willing to help" said Ashton.

"Well then, we have to move fast, major Anderson of the English navy, will soon ask commander Anthony Gibbs for help, not to wage a war, but some intellectual help with intelligence to find this ship that is anchored amongst us. May be they may be a positive enemy to us in some way" said Dale.

"Commander Anthony Gibbs will definitely give help to the English for they are our friends" replied Benn.

"But I need you personal help on this case" said Dale.

"OK I am in with you and your plans" said Doctor Ashton Benn.

Dale stretched his right hand to Benn for a handshake to seal his promise. It was welcomes then Dale said "I will count on you in a few minutes time" said Dale as he walked out of Benn's office.

"I will be here with you that is my promise, my dear buddy" said Benn as he rose from his chair to continue his job.

Chapter 17

By three o'clock that morning, Farouk together with Zabida, they once again evacuated their ship Allah Blessing to their small water craft to their destination to their camp on land.

The ship Allah Blessing had an easy access to the top of the ship to the water surface, then to their small water craft. From the bow they have a special built elevator that was stationary to the boat, this elevator began from a door way from the below floor, to get on and off their water craft, it rised to the second floor, then continued to raised to the third floor as its destination, so going up or down or to any one of the floor it was easy and fast.

This elevator was about four feet by six feet in size, so at this point captives could be taken with haste on board or out board without any problem. Thus to the small and fast water craft their job was handy and fast with a remote control to the elevators and doors.

However, the elevator was built in a special designed on the ship that it could not so easily recognized by onlookers, its engineers matched its looks like a modern style.

However by four o'clock the pair of half brother and sister as lovers were back at their medical camp to facilitate their functions, by this time they told themselves that they were doing well, nevertheless they will have to move fast for time was running on them with all those captives onboard their ship, as such maybe some one may notice some movements or something may go wrong so it is time for the ship "Allah Blessings" should set sail to its return destination as early as possible.

To their idea, almost their mission was completed and the only thing remain was to get their hands on Major Anderson Hudson, so this day they believed some how he will walk into their trap and that would be it. They knew that they had to be smart and skeptical for his daughter was their main bait to his re-action. All in all, Allah will give his blessings to them this day and as such as some miraculous means their fish will be trapped. Then their praises will be given to Allah the Almighty peace be unto him.

As the island of Haiti was busy as the ants, everyone were doing their job efficiently, so was Paul Saxon, he had made the deliver of food, water and clothing to their gang leader Kunta, to his members this was a fortune for them and their family to enjoy the spirit of bravery.

As the sun rises, Paul with haste and determination added another promise to them, thus they became more careful and dedicated to their job and to prove them selves as an established gang of power.

As the sun was rising to cover the island of Haiti, so was the tension for many. Kunta gang in full forces armed with their cutlasses confronted Don Diego "Scarface" gang, who were at all times armed for they too were paid well in food and water for a special job. Then the clash of weapons began to spark under the hot sun, thus the island of Haiti was soaked with more of its offspring blood.

The battlefield was fast and fierce. Kunta's gang outnumbered Scarface's gang for it was a surprise for them, so they fell victim in the bloody battle to Kunta hands.

For Scarface who new name was Abdulla, his wounded as casualties were taken to Farouk's medical camp. At once Zabida and Farouk get the message, things were not in their favour luck was running out.

Zabida decided to make her final booty to her ship and set sail the coming night as darkness gathered, thus Abdulla and his casualties was sent on board their ship "Allah Blessings". Abdulla and his gang was told they were going for special treatment and to take a good rest with sufficient medication with food and water, this on their recovery they would be back on land as healthy and fit individuals and to continue their fight.

Paul Saxon got the message so it was delivered to major Anderson Hudson, being as smart major for his survival in warfare he gained this position he began his trail, this he believed was the loose and open end for him to solve his mystery.

Onboard the English navy ship anchored in the Caribbean sea close to the island of Haiti, there was a color female Sergeant Pebbles Jones who was left in command, this was no warfare so in stead of major Lesa Clintwood to be in charge she was taken on land for there help was needed, however Sergent Pebbles was once again joined by major Lesa Clintwood for a special assignment.

Sergeant Pebbles was born and raised in Manchester England, she was the offspring of a Negro father and mothered by a white woman. Her father Scott Jones was an English navy Captain; ironically Pebbles took the blood of her father but looks of her mother. Before she joined the British army she was a black belt in karate, however as she joined the British army she chose to be a diver, to up kneep her athelitic body, as such she and her team of divers were left behind to protect the English navy ship.

By this time Sergent Pebbles was in her late twenties, slim and tall to rise six feet in height. Her beauty was various in merits. At her leisure time for fun, she would continued her combat training, in self defence, she was pretty as a swan, but in her line of duty she was ugly as sins. When She practice karate one could see the cruelty in her face as a mixed duel, this her father always proud of her. Pebbles also survived in the cold war in Iraq, above all any one could tell what she was, a deadly weapon for the English navy crew.

Major Lesa Clintwood had returned to take command over the English navy ship, at once Sergeant Pebbles and three of her colleagues of divers were specially briefed by Lesa, about her assignment below the water, their job was to find this enemy ship as fast as possible. Pebbles was in command, she was always a live surviver. Her motto, was fight to survival for there is no second chance, to attack or to die.

On this mission she and her team were fully armed, ready to hit below the water, she wore a knife to her left side while a powerful fish gun strapped to her right. So were her team. "To kill" was always her mission, she never accepted defeat. Her thoughts were her dead body will face defeat, once alive she must be the winner.

As Pebbles's team was about to descend below the blue waters of the Caribbean sea, lesa got the message from major Anderson "look for the small craft, that is at present taking some Haitian casualties" at once Pebbles and her team got the news, so they know what they were about to look for.

Pebbles and her team was scattered in a short distance from one another, they were to rise at intervals with only their eyes above the surface of the water to look for the special water craft.

Sometimes later, the team of divers saw their objective. Waheeda was the Captain of the small water craft, this was her second trip when she was spotted by the English divers. The divers with their head visible a little distance away were looking at Waheeda movements, as she stopped alongside the ship Allah Blessing, the elevator came down to the surface of the water.

The casualties were helped into the elevator, then quickly went upwards. Then stopped to the middle of the ship's height, then the door open as the elevator stand still for a short while, by this time Waheeda was making her way back to land.

As the elevator had spent some time on the middle floor of the ship, the door closed as the elevator went back to its position to the below floor.

The team of divers then headed back to the English navy ship to report to major Lesa. At once major Anderson was informed.

Immediately Major Anderson radioed the American commander Anthony Gibbs for help Major Anderson explain the situation to the American commander, they both agreed that these people were dangerous and there were many lives at stake so that thy have to act with precaution or else these terrorists may blow up this ship with will these people as hostage will die. This was their plan major Anderson formulate the plan while

Commander Gibbs who was in charge of the American war ship, they both put their few ideas together to be successful.

"How do you expected to take over this ship?" asked Commander Gibbs.

"My team of divers had already identified the location of the ship, so I have a plan to send them to work at once." said Anderson.

"What is this plan?" asked Gibbs.

"My diver will trim the fins of their propellers that if in case they decide to sailed away the propellers will be working but cannot push the ship" said Anderson.

"Suppose they decided to blow up the ship with all the victims?" asked Gibbs.

"Our divers will be in the water if they decided to escape, for these people will not commit suicide, because they are the educated leaders, they will betrayed the foolish one to kill their selves in a suicide bombers" said Anderson.

"How will we get in the ship?" asked Gibbs

"We will cut a hole in the ship a little above the water quietly, from above they would not know what is going on below, and then our crew will move in" said Anderson.

"Then how will we get these victims out of there to safety?" asked Gibbs.

"That part is a challenge, this we would both worked out an idea to get these captives, but those who are healthy and active we could used life jackets, with the help of our own crew they would within a few hundred feet get help up to one of our ship" said Anderson.

"That sounds good, by the way, try to be onboard my ship within a few minutes that we could matured a good plan before nightfall, because these terrorists are very clever, furthermore they usually move very swiftly when they change their plans so fast. In many cases a thousand of lives in no issue for them, once they stay alive to work on a next plan or movement." said Commander Gibbs.

"OK I will be there within a short while" said Major Anderson.

Major Anderson with haste as a commander in warfare waste no time to put things in place not to aroused no suspicions to his enemies.

Onboard the largest warship in the world, Major Anderson was met with Commander Gibbs and a few of his experienced team to draft out a plan to combat this situation.

It was agreed that the team of divers will consist of some experienced doctors, as there would be a great number of helpers on board, they all sat for a length of time to draft out a good plan for the advantages and disadvantages that the least mistake occur lives will be last and that was not what they were preparing for. It was all about saving these innocent lives to once again total freedom.

As their discussion went along it was agreed that Doctor Ashton Benn and Doctor Dale Mackintyre will be among the team. The operation will be led by major Anderson Hudson.

Also major Lesa Clintwood and Sergeant Pebbles Jones will consist of the team. To their conclusion they formulated a plan of a though crew that made out of streets fighters in combat.

Their operation was to begin immediately, so by night fall in the dark, they will be busy below the water as a school of sharks hunting for a hunting ground to feed on.

Chapter 18

Abu Farouk and the Angel of Death, Zabida, were planning for anything; if one plan changes then they will bargain amongst themselves for another once they were the winner. Things were going well for them from the beginning, but today things had changed. The inhabitants were in a battle which they loose, the two bosses knew the reason for this so they decided to grab, at the last peoples to full their ship for its booty. It was their plan.

When Abdulla (Scarface) and his gang suffered injuries some badly wounded as lifeless casulties it was Zabida's idea they began to work on. However they got the news that Kunta gang was working for someone else and they were spying on them, so there were an encounter of weapons exchange. But Zabida and Farouk had put their Mathematics and psychology together to solve their equation so their conversation went in to the future plan.

All in all the two of them work out things together, at last they came to a conclusion, Farouk advised Zabida "Prepare to leave tonight, then I will follow if not tomorrow, it is a guarantee it will be the next day"

"What do you mean by that?" asked Zabida.

"When you leave in the dark tonight, no one will arouse any suspicion, because your ship will sail in the night, no one will know your business because this camp will remain and function, then within twenty four hours you will covered a lot of miles" said Farouk.

"And why are you staying back for twenty four hours" asked Zabida.

"To get that English major" said Farouk.

"What is your plan to capture him?" asked Zabida.

"As you leave tonight, tomorrow I will befriend him, then invite him as a friend on my water plane, then after that God knows and you too." said Farouk.

"That sounds like a plan, he may believe we have one water craft, as our ship in that sea, so he may be interested to see what is going on onboard" said Zabida.

"I will also offer him assistance to find his daughter to lead him in to my trap" said Farouk.

"And if that does not work, what would you do? Why not fly your craft tonight with us?" asked Zabida.

"No! You sail first. I will try to look honest behind, then when everything look good and everyone suspicions is cleared as other ships are pulling out, so will I." said Farouk.

"OK so it is agreed upon that by nine tonight my ships propellers will begin to work" said Zabida.

"Yes, then we will meet in a few days" said Farouk.

"Do not push things too hard, if you can't get hold of that major in Haiti, then you will put your hands on him somewhere else" said Zabida.

"That is my mission to Haiti. I know the English government will send him here" said Farouk.

"But in my ship lies millions of dollars that we acquired within these few hours, why not leave him for a next trip" asked Zabida.

"That is your mission, I was here to help you, so that we could make money to finance our future project" said Farouk.

"Ok you know what you are doing, and then I will leave tonight for sure" said Zabida.

"Yes that is final, when you leave I will handle things different and leave as innocent as a saint who had given tremendous help to this island" said Farouk.

They were interrupted by Waheeda who told them that all was well and the scientist were onboard are doing well with their last cargo.

Major Anderson Hudson had met with Britney's manager Mr. Astor Jenkins to discuss the disappearance of Britney and her photographer Bill Samson. It was agreed that the news should remain silent for many reasons. He then met with Paul Saxon to used Kunta's gang to have eyes over Farouk's whereabouts, any help he needed he should contact the English army base, this major Anderson was agreed upon for Paul Saxon to handle this position for if the English army should keep eyes on Farouk medical camp, they would become suspicions, then his daughter life was in danger.

By evening major Anderson was on board the English navy vessel in full command.

Major Lesa Clintwood together with Sergeant Pebbles Jones and her three companions were gathered in front of Major Anderson in full command.

"Sergeant Pebbles you are in command of this mission, for you are a more experienced diver, major Lesa will be with you for any idea or advice, but this must be accomplished successfully" said Major Anderson.

"Yes Sir" replied his crew.

"The order is this!" said Major Anderson as everyone looked at him in attention carefully.

"Five divers are going down below that water, on your return, your success will determine our accomplishment, you are to search below that ship for all loop holes, when you are back each of you should know it like a map, make sure you all memorized it in your head, do you hear me!" said major Anderson.

"Yes Sir" roared the crew.

"Those propellers below that ship should be tightly wrapped with ropes to form two wheels not a propeller again. The reason for this is if they decided to put that ship in gear to move then propellers will only spin like wheels not pushing the boat. So in case while we are working below no one will get hurt, so by the time they realized what a is going on, our team of soldiers must be inside that ship. Get it!" roared Anderson.

"Clearly sir!" they roared.

"Any questions?" roared Major Anderson.

"How long do we have?" asked Pebbles.

"As snappy as you can" said Anderson.

"By what time do you expect the full team below that ship?" asked major Lesa.

"Before dark, tonight!" said Major Anderson.

"Can I ask a question, that I may grant permission?" asked major Lesa.

"Permission is granted" said Major Anderson.

"How do you expect to get inside the ship/" asked major Lesa.

"By cutting a small door above the surface of water" said Major Anderson.

Everyone was silent

Then Major Anderson said "This will be the help of the Americans, to get out all these hostages inside"

"That is all sirl" said Lesa.

"So then what are you waiting for? Move!" said Major Anderson.

Within a few minutes the team of divers were in full gear and ready, with their weapons, tools and ropes one by one they descended below the surface of the water for their mission.

With two coils of three quarters inches ropes, each coil tied to a small life bouy, that will enable the two coils of ropes to keep afloat below the waters, so it can be easily pull by divers. A boundle of rags clothings sealed in plastic bags also tied to a life bouy, this bundle of clothes was to stuff the propellers, which would bind with the ropes. With the help of the water current below they struggled their way to the mark ship "Allah Blessings". Major Lesa was ahead as a pilot fish.

Below the ship, in two pairs they began to work on each propeller while the fifth gave assistance when needed also to be alert for danger.

After a short moment the two propellers looked like two wheels with the ends of the ropes well bind and not to give away. With their signals they were busy in their assignment finishing binding the propellers they began this scouting to the bottom of the ship. They secured two strong tying places if needed to tie ropes for any help, this was found near to the propellers at the deck, and then at the bow they found another. This they knew will be needed that was why Major Anderson tells them to study below the ship as a map.

As they continued to explore the ship's bottom they were attracted to a school of fish feeding on an out let pipe, on checking what was the cause of that, they realized fresh blood was draining from the pipe thus the fishes were feeding on that. They then decided to find out the depth of the water that the ship was floating in, not to be astonished there were human skulls and bones scattered around the close vicinity of the ship at the sea bed.

Below that ship it was horrible and dangerous for large flesh eating fish will pass in a fast gush to grab at bait. Either a small fish or some particles of food to eat, above all the vicinity attracted living parasite all finding as some sort of feeding ground.

However at last they all had a map in their brains about the ship's bottom and its surroundings, as such they could answer any question to their superior or to anyone, and a full detail account could be given without hesitation.

Shortly after two hours of scouting, they had completed their mission and were climbing onboard the English navy ship to answer to major Anderson Hudson. There they explained to Major Anderson about the human skulls and bones, the pipe of blood oozing, Major Anderson then looked at them, his eyes trying to read their brains to focus on the map they had registered in their head.

At this point Major Anderson's head began to erupt, thinking about his daughter's safety, in the hands of these terriorests.

Major Anderson was interrupted by a soldier who said "major there is a call from Commander Anthony Gibbs from the American warship afloat on the water."

"Excuse me soldiers, have some rest and prepare for the next order" said Major Anderson.

Major Anderson went to answer the call from Commander Gibbs "Yes commander, I am ready to take orders from you" he answered.

"I have some good news for you" answered commanded Gibbs.

"Let it flow, please commander" answered Major Anderson.

"Mu crew was on the satellite working for some time, however they got it to work in their way, and guess what, they found the secret of the ship" said Commander Gibbs.

Major Anderson snappily cut in "what did they see on the ship?"

"Everything we wanted to know, the ship is made of three floors, the bottom floors is where all; the hostages is being held in cages as prison of war. Then the second floor is some thing like a hospital and the top floor is a luxurious living quarters" said commander Gibbs.

"Do you by chance see a white girl as a prisoner who supposed to be my daughter" Major Anderson snapped in, anxious for an answer.

"I think for one Doctor Dale recognized a female supposed to be your daughter" replied Commander Gibbs.

"Is she safe?" asked Major Anderson.

"Supposed to be, but Doctor Dale could tell you more about that, for he will join your ship very soon with other doctors to help. Replied Commander Gibbs.

"A team of my crew of divers were below that ship, so we have everything in place" said Anderson.

"We saw them on our screen, they had done a wonderful job" said Commander Gibbs.

"So you all saw everything about the ship?" asked Major Anderson.

"Yes we have laid out our plan, Sergeant Ashton Benn a good scientist and doctor will explain our plan, but you will lead the team" said Commander Gibbs.

"That is fine, I will definitively command the team, all I want is the support of your crew" said Major Anderson.

"It is all an easy mission, we have everything planned out, above all we will be over looking the operation on our screen, if help is needed there will be a second crew to be reinforced immediately" said Commander Gibbs.

Thank you commander" replied Anderson.

My support will be a success, by the way my crew will be there within a short while" said Commander Anthony Gibbs as he hang up the phone.

Chapter 19

Britney Hudson was trying to make herself comfortable in her small prison, however after the fatigue of the horrible event she had experienced then the victims and captive, the situation of this ship and, many things made her sick, weak in her concentration she fell into a long sleep during the day. But was awaken a few minutes ago to accept some dog food to keep her body alive with some strength.

To her idea these food were worst than the food given to prisoners, but she had no choice rather than to eat it to stay alive, for she realized if there is life here, there is a chance of freedom, then if she fall ill, these menace of scientists will change her life style for life.

As the below floor became to its normal life of the engines making a low noise, Britney was staring at Stacy Ann, whose eyes were looking back at her as she was comfortable in her mother's arms.

"Miss Britney are you ok" asked Stacy Ann

"Yes honey, I am fine" replied Britney

"You look confused, is something bothering you?" asked Stacy Ann.

"Just wondering about a few things" answered Britney.

"The doc is on your mind?" asked Stacy Ann.

Britney gave a little chuckle with a sad smile on her face and said "it is not about him"

"Will he come and get you?" asked Stacy Ann.

"How could he? He doesn't know where we are, I guess" she replied.

"What about your father? He is a major?" asked Stacy Ann.

"He will try his best, he is our only hope" said Britney.

"Do you believe we will get out of here?" asked Stacy Ann.

"Only God can help us1" said Britney.

"Do you believe in God?" asked Stacy Ann.

"Sometimes when in problems" replied Britney.

"Ok God will help us, because we are in problems" said Stacy Ann.

At this moment Lucy hugged Stacy to her breast and kissed her, then said "pray to God and he will help you when in problem, he is the savior of our soul, he is looking at us at present"

"Mama close your eyes and let us pray to him" said Stacy Ann.

Lucy tears began to drip as she whispered "oh dear Lord in heaven, have mercy upon us"

The three of them remain silent as they began to pray in their hearts.

On board the English navy ship there was a team with a plan and a mission, they knew what was their target, some had a view of the inside of the enemy ship so as entering they knew what they will find and how the inside was situated, however this team was commanding by their leader major Anderson Hudson.

The sun was about to hide its beauty behind the horizon, behind those high and huge mountains leaving its red glow as a last reflection, thus for the creatures who survived during the darkness it was the beginning of their break of sleep to their activities to find their feed, such was this mission to be busy in the darkness.

The American resque team joined the English, on their ship. Major Anderson was given a copy of the inside view of the ship "ALLAH BLESSING". It clearly showed the three stories and compartments of the entire ship. The English Major scaned it with his two nervious eyes then registered it in his visions.

He then give it to its resque team for them all to have a good look at it, so they all must know what their target look like. After a few minutes he made his final discussion over the map and their mission.

The genusis of this operation began to take birth, upon its success a few hundreds of innocent and vulunerable lifes were in their hands. With each soldiers on this mission knew their functions and target. Equiepted with their strength and bravery, they were all ready.

With the final command from Major Anderson they all began to hit the surface of the water, to each his own, victory shall be theirs. With them were two soldiers with two small tanks of morden equepments as cylinder of oxygen tanks to be used to cut the hole on the target ship. This morden mechisim could cut any thickness of steel sheets.

Ultimately the entire crew was like a school of sharks busy below the water. All the doctor had a little first aid kit straped along to their body, while the others with fish guns and knives as their weapons ready to attack and defend for they were all soldiers in combat as their career.

Zabida the Angel of Death with her half brother and lover Abu, who were at present her sex mate had to come to a decision of a final plan for everything was coming to a climax, as time was due to run out on them, such as luck with Britney and her partner in their captivity. This they knew will arouse suspicion for she was somebody in authority and an investigation will be launched some how and urgently, so they had their spies on Kunta's men secretly, also looking at major Anderson Hudson movements.

However, they got the news that the English Major had left for his ship, while the other soldiers had remained as volunteers rescue team.

All in all Farouk and Zabida both were intelligent scientists and maniacs, at last they came to one conclusion, to attack the Major in his ship. This will be a surprise for him so his defense will be weak.

Above all, Farouks personnel ship in the Caribbean water was not an ordinary ship. It was also a ship that cost a fortune, but for them the price does not count, once it was efficient in its job.

This ship was a water plane, specially designed and built for water and the sky, it does not have the capacity of accommodation a large crew, but for its purpose, it consists of space for two, four by four vehicles. These two vehicles both have a winch in front with a long coil of wire rope for its purpose.

Also it consisted of a small water boat of power, with also a winch with a coil of rope. The main purpose of these units for their own functions.

These combines units were so efficient on the water, land and air. To begin the water plane will land on the sea, it have a wide drop down door that consists of small wheels stationary on the drop down door for easy sliding, as the door is lowered to the water the water craft will easily slide to the open water, similarly to reload it, the wire rope will be tied inside the plane as the winch began to work, it will pull itself back inside easily by rolling on these small wheels.

The purpose of this craft was, as the water plane in the water, this water craft will pull the water plane close to any beach, then the two four by four vehicles will drive out, for help of the beach is muddy, they will tied the wire ropes to any tree on large rock, then it will pull itself to the safety to land.

On relanding the two four by four, it will pull itself back in to the water craft by their winches. Then the water boat would pull the water craft back to the deep waters. That was the purpose of these units with their wire ropes so they could be in any country or islands at any time.

So at present in Farouk's water ship was its Captain Hafies Sultan, who was also a scientist with his assistance of Asraf Hussain who was also a pilot and scientist. The two of them most of the time will be confined to this water plane and water craft but when comes to their real profession of science they were ready. Ultimately Farouk's team could enhance Zabida team at any time needed to be appropriate in full operation as a team of soldiers in warfare or to complete any mission, nothing was impossible for these combines team.

Above all Farouk and Zabida had to complete their mission and headed for their destination safely then to their other activities later on as life goes on. Their final decision that evening the four of them Farouk, Zabida, Waheeda and Fyzal will be on board Zabida ship Allah Blessing, then by dark, Farouk will make up a team of divers then they will head towards the English navy ship that was anchored in the Caribbean sea on the island of Haiti.

There will be major Anderson Hudson, who was at present their main objective and get hold of him as a captive will complete their mission.

Farouk's main idea was to get below that English navy ship with a team of divers, some how they will get onboard, if not they can't get on board, they would work out some way to plant a few devices as bombs to blow up this English Army Ship, to build these devices it was an easy task for Abu's team, then if luck on their side they will to put the American battle ship in to pieces.

Abu's suggestion was that the English army crew would be busy with their casualties, no one would expected intruders, because it was not expecting enemies. The main scenario of Abu's plans, they were seasoned terriorists where they have captured many victims of high ranks in high security already, this was a similar one, they will move like apache in the dark.

Most possible if things work his way, Zabida's ship will pull her anchors up and begin to hit the trail, while during the course of the night with his idea and determined his mission will be successful and the great major will be in his hand as a captive, in his water plane in the hands of the cruel Hafies Sultan and Asraf Hussain until some days late he will see his loving daughter. If not he will be in pieces like his ship in an explosion.

Hence both father and daughter will regret for they will both suffer in the eyes of one another, the major will bawl in pains of that torture to speak all the English secrets and his daughter will be raped by all the males of the Farouk's team, this will be their form of rejoice for a long while.

Meanwhile, back on the island, during that day mister Paul Saxon was trying to solve his mystery of the disappearance of his lover Mary Lucy and her daughter Stacy Ann.

Scarface's gang could not challenge Kunta's gang in a hurry, yet they wanted some kind of revenge on this master mind Paul Saxon so he was being carefully watched and followed.

As Kunta's gang was busy in their activities overturning every leaf and stones for answers for their pay was great, this was their encouragement.

Came evening Paul was by himself trying to pick up a little information at that may lead to some openings either for Britney or anyone missing it may lead to the same trail and as a result it may be a breakthrough this was because he was determined individual.

By himself, Paul was approached by a handful of Scarface men, they took advantage over him, as a result he became a bloody lifeless rag doll. He was then carried to their boss medical camp, these men knew their boss Farouk will be proud to have him in this condition, as they all knew he was the one causing the problems.

Evening came and Farouk's team of Zabida, Waheeda, Fizal and Farouk were ready for their mission to be started on the ship Allah Blessing, so Paul Saxon was taken with them to join the missing who he was looking for, thus he was only creating problems on this island.

Also that evening they made their final transport of cargoes of casualties consisted of human bodies.

Chapter 20

The operation below the ship Allah Blessing was in full command under major Anderson Hudson, thus it was overlooked by Commander Anthony Gibbs through the satellite unto his computer screens. Here if any thing went wrong, or deciding of changing in plan upon any unforeseen circumstances of an idea, Commander Gibbs would instruct Major Hudson on a radio set.

Major Hudson was informed about the elevator exit and entrance of the ship as their target, Sergeant Pebbles with Major Lesa with two other divers were standing guard by the elevator below the water. Sergeant Pebbles head was above the water, but below the ship, so she was not visible, here she could have a good look at the elevator while her partners were nearby below the water. They were all waiting to board or storm this target ship.

Other divers were scattered below the ship while Major Hudson had the team of the two welders cutting an entrance above the water, below the ship, while others were awaiting in haste to enter, but the opportunity had to go on slowly and safely for these terrorists could blow up the ship killing everyone including themselves for this was their faith, to commit suicide before being held captive and tortured.

Inside the ship Allah Blessing, Zabida and Farouk were having their final discussion. Zabida crew was made up of her fifteen scientists, they were building their plan, it was decided that Farouk will take six of her crew members, with the six added to Farouk and Fizal they will be a team of eight members to remain on the island for their mission.

Abu's team of eight will slide down the elevator in their diving suits and headed for their final plan to the English ship. While Zabida with her team of nine will sail away, but not in a haste, the elevator will remain to the water surface so within an hour and a half the team will return, thus the will used the elevator to get back up for their final plan if help is needed,

If they does not return within that time that means something went wrong at this point Zabida will make her decision as what to do, send help or to go along her journey, if possible the divers of Abu and his team will head for Farouk ship then call her on their telecommunication system to inform her next move.

Below the bottom floor sits Britney and others without any hopes of freedom. Paul was brought on to their presence then placed in a cage with a young lady who had occupied it already; it was a cage actually opposite Britney's. As Paul was placed in the cage with a female partner as his caretaker, the scientist who brought him said to the young lady "take care of his injuries, if he dies, you die!" with a serious look at the woman, as he leave.

"Oh my God the ship is already overcrowded" whispered Britney to herself.

As the captor left Britney whispered softly a little loud for Paul to hear her "Paul! Paul can you hear me?"

Paul began to raise his head to the whispering voice as he heard his name for someone in here is his friend.

Britney tried again in her whispering voice

"Paul, please look at me, is me Britney"

Hearing the name once again, Paul began to think looking directly at the cage the voice was coming from."

"Paul! Please gain you strength, we are all here" replied Britney in her whisper.

Paul could recnognised the acent of Britney's voice.

Britney once more whispered in a low voice. ''Paul!''

Paul looking at the cage in the dim light, from where the voice was coming from.

"Britney; what do you mean we are all here?" asked Paul in a hoarse and sick voice.

"Paul come to your sense please! With me is your lover Lucy and Stacy Ann." whispered Britney.

Hearing the name Paul with the help of his female mate tried to sit to have a good look in Britney direction for his body was bloody and in immense pains, his eyes becomes wide with only the whites showing as two white balls, he tried to speak as he whispered "oh my God, they have all of us as prisoners"

"Be strong Paul, we are safe" whispered Britney.

"Lucy! Lucy! Can you hear me, if you can, I love you" whispered Paul.

"Me too Paul, I love you" whispered Lucy.

"Oh my God Lucy, I looked everywhere for you, please help me God here I find her that we can't do nothing to help one another" whispered Paul.

"Paul be quiet and be strong take a rest and pray God will help us" whispered Britney.

"Your father's men will attack this ship at any time, they are planning to get you out of here" said Paul.

"My father knows where I am?" asked Britney.

"Yes. He leave this morning to seek help form the Americans to set you free" replied Paul.

Hearing this words Stacy Ann became alive in a new world, so she interrupted Britney by saying "Miss Britney your dad is coming for you, will he help us all"

Britney looked at her and said directly "He is an English navy Major and his duty is to save all of us, not me alone."

"Will Doctor Dale come with them to help us?" asked Stacy Ann.

Britney looked at her in puzzlement why was she asking these questions. Then replied "I don't know honey"

"Miss Britney, do you love Doctor Dale?" Asked Stacy Ann.

"Why do you ask me that?" Asked Britney.

"I asking, do you love him?" yes or no!" asked Stacy.

Britney was looking at Stacy thinking how to answer to her questions.

Stacy Ann once again said "Please say yes you love him;

'' Yes, I love him he is a nice doctor" Replied Britney in a cool voice.

"Stacy Ann what are you asking me honey, at this time we need help" answered Britney.

"God will not come but he will send your dad and Doctor Dale to help us;" Answered Stacy Ann.

"Ok if he comes to help us then I love him" answered Britney.

"Ok miss Britney, if God sends him to help us, then promise me you will Mary him" said Stacy.

With these words Britney remembered the horrible words of Farouk and Zabida then the situation there in at present, then if help comes that is their freedom, then she rather to marry Doctor Dale than to be sold as a slave on a prostitute, Britney then closed her eyes and open and said to Stacy "yes I promise I will marry him if he love me"

"Ok miss Britney you promise God you will marry him because God will send him to help us all" said Stacy.

"Yes! I promise God I will marry him if God helps us" replied Britney.

"Well I will pray to God to send Doctor Dale to help us, will you mamma pray with me?" said Stacy Ann.

"Yes certainly pray with you for help to come" said Lucy.

"Ok miss Britney, everyone on this ship will pray to God to send help, will you join us?" said Stacy.

"Sure! Let us begin" said Britney.

As they all once more closed their eyes and began to pray in silence to God for help.

Farouk and his diving team by this time were ready to take the water, as they were in their full gear of diving suits and equipment, commander Gibbs, had send his message to major Hudson to look out for light divers who will be soon descended to the water through the elevator. Major Hudson at once leave his command to sergeant doctor Ashton Benn as soon as the entrance is open to take control inside the ship to help the patients and captives that needed medication. The major then began his dive to catch up with sergeant Pebbles and major Lesa and others to take control.

The elevator descended to the surface of the water, all the scientists of divers believed they knew their mission and destiny, but this time they are going to meet Allah for their sins.

Sergeant Pebbles saw the elevator coming down with the team of divers so she descended below the surface of the water to alert her partners.

They were below waiting for a combat the first diver came with his feet first, then to take balance for the mission. As he came below the water two pairs of hands caught hold or his feet, then pull him deeper, it was two late to give a signal. As the first was pulled deeper struggling with his feet in surprise, his oxygen hose was cut away from this face mask, and then he felt a blade in his stomach then his back to the kidney.

Similarly as the second diver was below the surface of the water, similarly was his fate. Within a few seconds the first pair of divers had finished off Farouk's first divers they rose to take control of Farouk's third diver. So it went on with Pebbles and Lesa and other mates taking advantage, until Farouk finally was the last diver from the elevator to descend below the surface of the water, his fate was similar.

Ironically Farouk's team became a failour as they fell easy victims to Lesa and Pebbles team that was the end of their mission for life, for below the surface of the water their blood began to flow.

They will met with allah to determine how much virgins they will receive in heavens as the terrorist believes more wrong things as evil they did it is more they will receive in their own fantasy of belief. But only the true and loving God will foresee their fate's when for surely the devil or evil; God will receive them in eternity.

However, as Lesa and her partners were making their way to finish off Farouk, Major Andersons was by their side, he signaled them to let go of him, he quickly unmasked him, then re-surfaced him above the water. Major Anderson realized he yet had some life, also he realized that he was the leader of this mafia so he quickly signaled one of the divers for a doctor to help.

This was because of his daughter Britney was not found on this ship he will have to answer or to lead them to her safety. Yet again major Anderson believed that death was too easy for him, he should suffer more pains in the law for the crimes he had participated in. He was immadetely carried away by two divers to the English navy ship for medication, with maybe a punctured lungs or kidney from Pebbles or Lesa, for they were professionals in the trade of death of their enemies for them to survive, however such is life in combat, no one want to suffer or to die.

Major Anderson Hudson a warfare dog was very experienced in his missions of attack to save his prisons waste no time, thus he ordered sergeant Pebbles and major Lesa with four other soldiers, as divers to follow him, they took to the elevator, at once he realized the elevator was self controlled with all the buttons alive to take them to any floor of the ship.

Without hesitation as the team of soldiers boarded the elevator and began travelling upwards, towards the top floor of the ship. Passing the first and second floors respectively to stop at the end of the third floor.

As the elevator stopped at its destination major Anderson looked at his team of soldiers, in their faces, he realised they were eager to get inside to do some actions. For they had faced death and encounter this situation at many time in their careers.

Major Anderson pressed the button to enter the top floor the electricity door slid open, its entrance was by the luxurious bathing pool. At this moment Major Anderson had to make a quick decision for his mission to be successful, he gave his signs to his group, six would enter while one will take back the elevater to the surface of the water, so it will be more easer for the resque team to enter the ship.

There sit the Angel of Death Zabida. As the door slid open her eyes were in contact of her intruders, Major Lesa Clintwood realized who she was, so with out hesitation she rushed to her followed by sergeant Pebbles Gomes. Zabida was quick to her feet in her self defense position as she was trained as a karate expert, so were her two opponents. At this moment major Anderson signaled to the other soldiers to follow him.

He knew Lisa and Pebles will take good care of her, so he and the others had to be quick to find the others, in the mean while he knew by this time the first floors will be flooded with the combine force of the English and American soldiers, so he decided to move forward to his enemies who were on the top floors. According to the plan of the vessel readings, the second floor will consisted of the kind of hospital.

Apparently Zabida was a good judo and karate fighter, however so was her opponents Lesa and Pebbles. Zabida was dancing well with her spin kicks to her target. If her attackers were amateurs they would have fell easy victims to her experience in fighting.

Lesa in front of Zabida placed a spin kick to Zabida face, she easily blocked it with her two hands, at the said time Pebbles from behind of her spin low with a kick to her feet to trip Zabida to the floor, but she was so good that so fast she leapt in the air as she landed back to the floor, she automatically bounced back in the air with a summersault, so agile as a monkey, then a fly kick so fast that she caught Pebbles to her face. Pebbles rocked back shaking her head as a fierce bull, by this time Lesa moved in as a cat with two fast jabs that caught Zabida to her back to her kidney area.

As fast as a mongoose Zabida leap to the floor, then as a snake she got hold of Lesa two feet, Lesa fell off balance, by this time Pebbles got balance and rocked a good spin kick with good average that connect Zabida once more to the kidney area. Zabida was so active that she open her two hands in the air like Bruce lee spranging as a leopard.

Lesa looked at Pebbles in opposite directions, in heavy concentration they both made an eye contact, both gave a nod a signal to each other then charged into Zabida. As the two of them charged into Zabida, she made a summersault in the air then in to the swimming pool, both Lesa and Pebbled leapt behind her.

Zabida was so fast that she within seconds on the other side of the pool step mapping her way out of the pool for an escape. Pebbles were behind her heels, she held to her feet while Zabida was trying to kick her off. By this time Lesa was out of the pool like a dolphin as fast as the lightning, in a judo styling Lesa place a solid elbow behind Zabida neck, thus she felt weak with dizziness, but yet struggles on, out of Pebbles grip to the ship floor and out of the pool step.

Once again the three experts were in combat, but Zabida was fading. Lesa made a fake attack towards Zabida, but held back, Zabida in defense went for a deadly blow to her attacker, but nothing came as she came off balance, Lesa then confirmed her action caught Zabida a next kick to the kidney. At once she rocked in pain, at the said moment Pebbles made a leap to her enemy, she got hold of her head with her two hands, Pebbles was going to break her neck in a fast jerk. Lesa saw it then shouted "no" as Pebbles stop her motion and looked at Lesa, Lesa came with a solid backwards kick to Zabida back, and it connected to her spins.

Zabida collapse as a cripple to the floor at once, groaning in pains, Pebbles was determined to continued her motion of breaking Zabida neck, but Lesa said "her spine is broken she is a cripple, hurry lets go we will find her right here when we need her" as Lesa briskly move away. Pebbles let go of Zabida as she lay lifeless on the floor as a cripple snake in her eyes were venom, with her two hands Zabida tried to move, but it was of no use. Pebbles quickly leaves and followed Lesa.

Chapter 21

Upon the surface of the water of the Caribbean sea, the combine force of the American and English were eager to get in that enemy ship, for some of their enemies were below the surface of the water lying on the sea bed talking to Allah about the good things that they achieved in life by robbing and stealing. At present they had held members of the innocent lives as captives in prison cages. They had also butchered humans, when they steal their lives these were the good these terrorists had done in the fate of Allah their so called God.

However, the God sent people are like shark to kill these demons and to restore freedom to these innocent captives as a good and great God wanted. So with the good and great God by these attacking soldiers side they were about to gain victory.

They had cut and entrance to the below floor of this devout ship of Allah blessing. The first to enter was Sergeant Ashton Benn followed by Doctor Dale Mackintyre; they had seen a photo footage of the ship layout onboard the American war ship, so definitely they knew what they were looking for and the image of the Devil ship insides. While others took to the evevator that was functioning well.

Lucy, Paul and all mates, Bill Samson also with some other joined in with their prayers, it started from their hearts, then to whispered at last it developed into a chain of prayers that the sounds of their prayers developed to an echoing noise, this caused two of the scientists to burst open the door to the bottom floor to quiet these captives in some way, either by some penalty of a good beating or even their death.

This situation Benn and Dale took advantage upon. As the two scientist came down in a rage both Dale and Benn got hold of one each from back, within minutes their throat were slit with a sharp soldiers knife leaving their body to jump on the ships floor liker the way Muslims do to halal any meat, leaving the animals blood to drain in a long death.

By this time the below floor was crowded with American and English doctors and soldiers. Dale rushed to Britney cell; her eyes were close with her mouth singing her prayers. Dale was shaking the cell door shouting "Britney! Britney! Wake up! Britney could hear me!"

Britney heard Dale's voice but thought that it was a dream, by this time another soldier with a tool burst the lock, Dale quickly pulled the gate open got hold of Britney to her two shoulders shaking her "Britney! Britney! Please for God sake open you eyes, it's me Dale"

At that said time Stacy Ann prison door was swing open by Doctor Ashton Benn. He had learnt about his daughter through Doctor Dale. Benn had swing the prison door wide open held Stacy onto his stomach in a hurry, Stacy Ann clung to the soldier for safety not knowing that the soldier was her real father, she open her eyes and looked at Britney, at once she recognized Dale handsome face, Stacy Ann began to shout "Doctor Dale you came for miss Britney"

Dale looked at her with a smile then said "you recognized me"

"Yes I must recognize you, Miss Britney said she will marry you if God help us" said Stacy

"Yes honey, God had sent us to help you" replied Dale

"Will you marry Miss Britney", asked Stacy.

By this time Britney opened her eyes to see Doctor Dale had her in a standing position trying to get her out of her sleep, as she recognized Dale Britney scramble to him in a hug, then whispered in his ears "Dale, I love you"

"That is fine with me, are you ok" said Dale

Stacy Ann again butt in "Miss Britney you promised me and God that you will marry Doctor Dale if he came to help us, please Miss Britney"

Britney once again whispered in Dale's ears not to release her embracement "Yes Dale I will marry you, I promised Stacy that, will you make me your wife. I love you Dale, please say yes"

Dale drew Britney closer to his stomach as the two hearts beat becomes one then said to Stacy

"Yes Stacy Ann, Miss Britney will be my wife"

"Then I will come to your wedding" said Stacy.

"That soldier that you are hugging is your father doctor Ashton Benn, he will take you to our wedding" said Dale.

Stacy took a good look at Benn face and ask

"Are you my real papa?"

"Yes" said Benn shaking his head in sympathy.

"Why you leave me and mama?" asked Stacy Ann.

"That is a along story" said doctor Benn.

On the upper floor sergeant Pebbles and major Lesa had just cripple the Angel of Death Zabida leaving her to crawl like a snake looking to inject the last deadly venom.

While major Anderson Hudson and his team of three remaining soldiers at that time came face to face with Katija Ali the Captain of this devil ship Allah blessing, Katija with another scientist whom was her lover were having some coffee in the ship's dining room, seeing their invaders enter the dining room, they were once in action for these scientists were warriors they were all marcial arts experts, major Anderson and his three colleagues realized this, as Katija and her other mate began to shape their body for an attack and defense.

Katija like a wild cat sprang at major Anderson, she was a furious and fast that Anderson had no choice but as a soldier in the defense went for his knife, the knife had slice Katija below her left ribs, but yet she got hold of Anderson hand, trying to break his wrist, Anderson made a flick like an alligator in the water, Anderson fell to the ground while Katija was on her feet.

Anderson spring to his feet as fast as an agile old tom cat to save his old life, while the knife went to its own way, but he had to defend himself, Katija was bleeding but was maneuvering Anderson in any attack. Katija and her lover partner were too good for Anderson and his team, but they were trying to defend themselves to stay alive hoping for Lesa and Pebbles to join them to strengthened their team. Anderson and his team will be wiped out by Katija and her partner, however Anderson and his two soldiers were only defending them selves against these two experts, trying to stay alive until help comes, which was due any time.

Then after a few minutes Lesa and Pebbles took over the attack on Katija for she was fiercer and swift than the others, the battle went on two against six.

Within a few minutes Katija became a cripple like Zabida, Katija became a cripple with her spinal broken as a trick of Lesa, but Pebbles with the help of her team broke the other's neck.

In the middle floor four remaining scientists were busy in their doctoring works on the held captives. The American and British soldiers as a full battalion in combat of attack swarm the second floor with knives and fish gun in hands ready to kill held the scientists at fish gun point as captives.

By this time major Anderson team had searched the top floor for enemies but found none, so they descended to the second floor to find out the four remaining scientist fell captive.

"How much soldiers onboard this ship?" demanded Major Anderson to the captives.

No answer came from them.

"Let's get some cruelty as these helpless people are enduring at present" belched Major Anderson with venom in his voice.

At that moment a fish gun rubber sing a sound and an arrow stick in one of the terrorist eyes, he shiver backwards and fall."

"Nine" snapped one of them.

"Is this organization have any linkage" asked Anderson.

No one answered

"Let them speak" said Major Anderson.

A knife went in one of the terrorist mouth ripping the skin of his mouth on both sides of his jaws, he groaned in pains.

A next knife was forced in the other mouth top rip his tongue off, he spit out blood with a piece of his tongue.

The last one who was speaking began to speak, at last nothing became a secret for the combine force of American and English.

At last this devil ship Allah Blessing was in the command of major Anderson Hudson, the Captain and his crew fell captives in this major hands to stand trials of their actions and crimes.

Commander Anthony Gibbs was aware what went on, but later that night he was also in command to capture Farouk water plane piloted by Captain Hafies sultan and his companion Asraf Hussain.

As Major Anderson got the secret of this water plane in command by Farouk, he radioed Commander Gibbs, with two armed navy air craft above Farouk's water plane his two men showed no fight but gave up.

At last the entire Zabida and her remaining crew together Farouk's men were in the hands of the English and American soldiers they were no more bosses but became prisoners.

At last all the captives were treated and release. For the ship "Allah Blessings" was swamped with English and American doctors and scientists to help in some way, thank God for the English and American to help the helpless once innocent people who really needed help but was betrayed by these terrorists.

Mary Lucy gave Stacy to this couple free heartedly for if not for them she and her daughter might have been sold as some slave.

Most of all Mary Lucy was free to visit Britney and Dale to see Stacy Ann at any time

THE END

Printed in the United States
By Bookmasters